FAR FROM DESTINED

A Promise Me Novel

CARRIE ANN RYAN

FAR FROM DESTINED
A PROMISE ME NOVEL

By
Carrie Ann Ryan

FAR FROM DESTINED
A Promise Me Novel
By: Carrie Ann Ryan
© 2020 Carrie Ann Ryan
ISBN: 978-1-950443-93-2
Cover Art by Sweet N Spicy Designs
Photograph by Wander Photography

Praise for Carrie Ann Ryan

"Count on Carrie Ann Ryan for emotional, sexy, character driven stories that capture your heart!" – Carly Phillips, NY Times bestselling author

"Carrie Ann Ryan's romances are my newest addiction! The emotion in her books captures me from the very beginning. The hope and healing hold me close until the end. These love stories will simply sweep you away." ~ NYT Bestselling Author Deveny Perry

"Carrie Ann Ryan writes the perfect balance of sweet and heat ensuring every story feeds the soul." - Audrey Carlan, #1 New York Times Bestselling Author

"Carrie Ann Ryan never fails to draw readers in with passion, raw sensuality, and characters that pop off the page. Any book by Carrie Ann is an absolute treat." – New York Times Bestselling Author J. Kenner

"Carrie Ann Ryan knows how to pull your heartstrings and make your pulse pound! Her wonderful Redwood Pack series will draw you in and keep you reading long into the night. I can't wait to see what comes next with the new generation, the Talons. Keep them coming, Carrie Ann!" –Lara Adrian, New York Times bestselling author of CRAVE THE NIGHT

"With snarky humor, sizzling love scenes, and brilliant, imaginative worldbuilding, The Dante's Circle series reads as if Carrie Ann Ryan peeked at my personal wish list!" – NYT Bestselling Author, Larissa Ione

"Carrie Ann Ryan writes sexy shifters in a world full of passionate happily-ever-afters." – *New York Times* Bestselling Author Vivian Arend

"Carrie Ann's books are sexy with characters you can't help but love from page one. They are heat and heart blended to perfection." *New York Times* Bestselling Author Jayne Rylon

Carrie Ann Ryan's books are wickedly funny and deliciously hot, with plenty of twists to keep you guessing. They'll keep you up all night!" USA Today Bestselling Author Cari Quinn

"Once again, Carrie Ann Ryan knocks the Dante's Circle series out of the park. The queen of hot, sexy, enthralling paranormal romance, Carrie Ann is an author not to miss!" *New York Times* bestselling Author Marie Harte

To those searching for a second chance.

Far From Destined

New York Times and *USA Today* bestselling author Carrie Ann Ryan continues her sexy new contemporary stand-alone series with a broken heart and the shattered soul that can heal them both.

Macon Brady remembers every moment he lay on the ground, a bullet in his chest, his life bleeding out with each pulse. Yet his nightmares aren't the only thing keeping him up at night.

Dakota Bristol left her ex with nothing but the clothes on her back and her child in her arms. She's been hurt before and wants nothing to do with the shadows in Macon's eyes. The problem? Her son loves him, and the more time she spends with the man, the more she's afraid she'll come to love him just as much.

Danger always comes back to haunt those who run. It was a lesson Dakota learned before. Now, it might be the man she refuses to fall for who makes the greatest sacrifice of all.

Chapter 1

Macon

I DUCKED THE PUNCH TO THE FACE, THEN CAME OUT swinging, my fist connecting with the jaw of the man in front of me. He let out a grunt, stumbling back. I hit again, and again, jabbing, going for his ribs. I threw a cross, an uppercut, continued moving until I was pulled away, my hands lifted in the air, and announced the winner.

Sweat slicked my body, and I heaved out a breath, running my hand over the pebbled scar on my chest— the memory that would never fade, the flesh that would never fully heal.

Anyone who understood scars knew where the marred flesh had come from, and if they didn't know me, they likely figured I was some kind of badass to have it. They thought it was a scar of pride, not one of fear.

Those that knew me understood I never wanted to remember that pain, never wanted to remember bleeding out and begging for help.

I never begged. I never asked for help.

Only as I lay there dying, wondering what would happen when I closed my eyes for the final time, not seeing my life flash before my eyes as others promised, I knew I'd run out of time.

I hadn't been strong. I had been weak.

I was weak no longer.

As my trainer put his arm around my shoulders, I knew I would come back to the ring and trounce anybody I could. I would win as many times as I could to prove that I wasn't weak.

It didn't matter that the people here didn't know me. It didn't matter that these were sanctioned fights and I wasn't in some underground shit that would end up hurting me in the end. I knew that what I was doing was dangerous.

And I didn't give a fuck.

I was just so goddamn tired.

Every cut on my wrist, every bruise on my jaw told me that I was here.

That no matter what happened, I would still be here.

That the scar on my chest wasn't the only thing that

mattered when it came to who I was.

"Doing a good job, Brady."

I nodded, pushing my hair from my eyes. "Thanks," I said, spitting into the bucket next to me as I pulled out my mouthguard. No blood this time, so I counted that as a win.

"You still up for just boxing? Or, we could start training in mixed martial arts."

I shook my head. "Don't think I'm that flexible." I laughed, while one of the ring girls raked her gaze over my body before meeting my eyes.

"Oh, I'm sure you're quite flexible," she purred, winking before sauntering off.

"I'd like a piece of that," Bob said, and I shook my head.

"She's married," I replied with a laugh, wiping my face with a towel.

"So? Didn't stop her from giving you a look like she wanted to go down on her knees in front of you."

"True, but that's just for show. Her husband could kick my ass."

"You've met the guy?" Bob asked as we made our way back to the training room so I could shower before heading home.

"Yes, and he could kick all our asses."

It was a lie for her benefit. Her husband was an IT guy who worshiped the ground she walked on. I only knew that because I had walked her to her car once to make sure she was safe in the dark, something *I* wasn't even comfortable with these days—not that I told anybody that.

Her husband had been late showing up to make sure she got to her car safely and skidded into the parking lot right when I was there.

He was all of a hundred and ten pounds soaking wet, glasses falling off his face, and his hands shaking, but he had stood up to me. I remembered smiling and lowering my head to explain to him what I was doing.

I liked the guy. We had exchanged numbers, and I was always there to make sure his girl made it to her car unharmed. She could take care of herself, but it was always smart to make sure that more than one person watched your back.

Of course, I hadn't been alone when I was shot, but you couldn't fight a gun with a fist.

It sure as hell seemed like I was trying these days.

"I'm off after I rinse the grime away," I said as I stripped out of my shorts and headed to the shower. "I've got to work in the morning."

"Got to go save those kittens," Bob sneered, and I flipped him off, unwrapping my hands as I turned on the water. My open wounds stung, and I cursed. This place had a doctor on call, but he was a jackass and didn't like me. That meant I'd either have to go to the emergency room or have my partner at my vet clinic help me if I needed stitches.

I looked down at my hands and figured I was safe there. I didn't have any deep cuts on my face, so I counted that as a win, too.

No stitches today, just ice, and then a beer later.

"You up for another fight next week?" Bob asked, looking down at his phone.

"No, got a family thing. I'll let you know when I need another round."

"You say that as if you're just using it as an excuse to punch somebody and not make money."

I didn't bet on myself. Actually, I didn't bet at all. All I did was fight, trying to get some of the rage under control. Honestly, I didn't know why I was doing this, and I knew I was probably going to hurt myself in the end, but my brothers and sister didn't know what I was doing. Nobody did.

I was just fine with that. If they knew I was fighting like this, they'd drag me home and yell me into submission.

Sometimes, I felt like I was weak enough to fall right into the plans others made for me. The person I was before I was shot. I was done being that guy. That man cried out for help and never got it. He pushed his brother away to save the girl rather than saving himself.

I wouldn't be that person anymore.

"Okay, man, just let me know when you're ready to fight again. I like it when you come in. You get shit done, and you don't whine about it."

"I do my best," I said dryly.

"Yeah, I think you do. It's probably why I like you. Stay safe, and don't fight anywhere but here. You don't want me to have to put you on an actual contract."

I snorted and shook my head. "I don't have that much of a death wish," I muttered.

"Good, kid. Don't get one now."

I nodded, then finished showering before drying off and pulling on my clothes. I didn't have much with me. I always worried that someone was going to steal my shit. Though tonight, nobody else was with me here. The guy I had fought had his own room, and we simply nodded at each other as we walked away. I liked Dave. He was a good guy. We both just tended to take out our rage on each other. Next time I saw him, we'd get a beer, though we didn't have much in common outside of the ring. And that was just fine with me.

I made my way to my car, grateful that everybody else had gone home, and nobody seemed to be around. I didn't want to have another conversation.

I was so tired of talking, pretending that everything was okay when it wasn't.

I had to go back to my normal life tomorrow and pretend I was fine, that I wasn't stressed out or repeatedly having nightmares about being shot. The fact that I could still hear Hazel screaming in my dreams was something I should probably tell somebody, but I wasn't going to. Not anytime soon, anyway.

Not when everything hurt.

I looked up at the sound of someone next to my car and froze, my fists clenching at my sides. I swore I could hear the cock of a gun, but then it was gone. The person in front of me was one of the last people I wanted to see.

"So, you want to tell me what the fuck you're doing?" my younger brother, Nate, asked, a scowl on his face.

"None of your fucking business," I countered, pushing past him to my car. "Where the hell are you parked?"

"I got a lift here. Heard you were fighting from a buddy who recognized you and texted me to get my ass here. I thought I should be able to drive your car back to your place if I had to carry you out of there."

"I take it you were inside?"

"Yep."

"Then you know there's nothing to worry about," I growled.

"Whatever you say. But we still need to talk."

"We don't." Shame crawled over me, and I hated myself. What had Nate seen? Would he tell everybody else? Jesus Christ, I couldn't do this right now.

Or ever.

"Come on, we're going to get some coffee, and we're going to talk about this."

"I don't need to talk about this," I said.

"We do. I'm not going to tell the others, but you and I need to talk. I don't care if you get pissy about it, but you're my brother, and I love you. And you're going to fucking listen to me."

"Nate."

"No. I'm done. Come on. We're going to go get some coffee."

Worry slid over me. "Where exactly are we getting coffee?

"You know where we are going." Nate paused and gave me a knowing glance. "If it helps, she's not working tonight."

I swallowed hard, trying not to think her name. "I don't know what you're talking about."

"Whatever. You're not very good at lying, you know."

"And you're driving me because I don't want to call my Uber."

"I can't believe you fucking Ubered here," I said, knowing that Nate was stubborn enough that he wouldn't let this go.

"I do what I have to do. Now, come on, I want coffee and a Danish."

"Danishes are for breakfast. She's probably not going to have them at her place."

"She might. And look at you, thinking of her instead of the shop."

"Fuck you," I growled, tossing my bag into the back before getting into my truck and starting the engine.

I headed to the Boulder Bean and parked in the back, grateful there was a space. The fight had been an early one, and they had closed up for the night since it was still a weekday. That meant the bakery was still open, despite the owner not being there.

At least, I hoped she wasn't here. I wasn't sure if I could face her all bruised and aching like this. Who was I kidding? I wasn't sure I could face her at all. And that was part of the problem.

We made our way into the café, taking a seat near the window. I didn't want my back to the door. Nate didn't seem to mind, but he did notice the hesitation. Regardless, he just gave me a look before shaking his head.

"I'm going to get us some coffees. What do you want?"

"Just a regular. Black."

"You're so boring," Nate said, grinning, though it didn't reach his eyes. He was worried about me.

And I was fucked.

"Thanks for the brew," I growled. He made his way

to the counter, the two of us occupying one of the two full tables in the café. The place was about to close soon, and I knew I should've just gone home. I could have even taken Nate with me so we could hash things out, but even though I wouldn't admit it, I'd wanted to come here on the off chance that I'd see her.

Because I was a fucking glutton for punishment. If I weren't, maybe I wouldn't be in the ring at all. Things wouldn't hurt as much as they did. Hell, I just wanted things to get back to normal.

I wanted to see her.

Only she wasn't here. And even if she were, she'd likely take one look at me and run, just like she always did.

"Macon?" a familiar voice asked. I froze, my whole body snapping to attention, my throat going dry.

I looked up to see her. Her dark hair was pulled away from her face in a messy bun, her creamy complexion rosy after a long day, her thick black glasses perched on the tip of her nose as if she had been reading and hadn't wanted to bother with her contacts. The fact that I knew she wore contacts most of the time should probably worry me, but it didn't.

Because I was a masochist when it came to Dakota, the woman I couldn't have, the female who wanted nothing to do with me. She had made it very clear that she didn't want me in her life, and yet, all I did was want more.

Because I was a fucking loser.

"Hey, Nate's getting me some coffee."

She studied my face as if waiting for me to say more. "Okay, you want to tell me what happened?"

"Nothing," I lied.

"You have blood on your knuckles and a bruise on your jaw. What happened? Who hurt you?"

I heard the fear in her voice and wanted to kick myself. I shouldn't have come here, even on the off chance that she would be here. It didn't matter that I wanted to see her.

Because I knew she was running from something. Given what had happened to our friends, and what she never spoke about when it came to her past, seeing me bruised would only bring back the horror of what neither of us wanted to talk about.

I was going to hell, and it was my own damn fault.

"Nothing. Just a long day."

"At work? You're saying a dog or a cat did this?"

"I do work with large animals sometimes if I have to go out to a farm and one of the other vets I know needs help." It wasn't a lie, but not the truth today.

"So, a cow did this, then?" she asked, and I shook my head.

"I'm fine, Dakota. Don't even need stitches."

"And because you're a vet, you can tell that?" she asked.

"Yes, I guess that's a good reason for me to know," I said, knowing I sounded like an asshole.

She shook her head, her glasses falling down her nose. I wanted to reach out and move them back. I didn't.

"What the hell, Macon? Who did this to you?"

"Nobody. I said I'm fine. Let's not talk about it."

She studied my face for a long moment before shaking her head, disappointment plain. "Why are you fighting?" she asked, and I wanted to curse.

"Dakota."

"No, I see your knuckles. You've clearly hit someone. And you want to hang out with Joshua?" she asked, her voice sharp even as she kept it quiet so nobody else could hear.

"Dakota." I needed to fix this. Somehow, I had to remedy this.

"No. I don't know what's going on with you, but you better stay away from my son. And me." Then she turned on her heel and went back to the office, leaving me sitting there, wondering what the fuck was wrong with me.

Nate came back with two to-go cups, a sad expression on his face.

"I honestly didn't know she would be here."

"It's fine."

"It's not."

"It is. Come on, let's just go." I took the coffee from Nate, nodded at him, and then left the building. The bell over the door echoed in my head, sounding like a fucking gunshot. I tripped over my feet, the coffee sloshing out of the cup, and cursed, not even feeling the heat.

"Fuck, are you okay?" Nate asked from behind me.

"I'm fine. Let's just go. I'll take you home."

"We still need to talk."

"You know, I think I've had enough talking for the night."

"Macon."

"No, you got what you wanted. Everyone's going to know that I'm a fucking asshole, and that's fine."

"That is not what I wanted. I wanted to make sure you were okay."

"I'm fine. As you can see, everything is just dandy. I'm scaring women and children, to the point where she's never going to talk to me again. But it doesn't matter, does it? Because it's not like she ever wanted to before."

"Macon."

Sweat covered my body as my hands went clammy, and I did my best to catch my breath, the sound of the gun cocking filled my ears again, the taste of blood in my mouth as if it just happened, the scream echoing in my head as Hazel shouted my name.

"I need to get home."

"Okay, I'll get you there."

"I need to go home," I repeated.

"I've got you. I'm driving. We're going."

He led me to the truck, and I got in, making sure the coffee was in its holder before covering my face with my hands and trying to catch my breath.

"I'm sorry," my little brother whispered.

"Not your fault. I'm the asshole."

"You're not."

"Then why does it feel like I am?"

"You're not," he repeated. "She'll talk to you again. She's just had a tough couple of days."

"Why?" I asked, giving him a sharp look. "What happened?" I hated that I was so protective of Dakota. She didn't want me in her life. She'd made that perfectly clear. Only I needed to help her fix things despite that she hated it when I tried. That was on me, and I was usually better at giving her space.

"It's just busy with the café, I think. I don't know for sure. It's just what I overhear from the girls. We're all one big group. We'll make it work. She's not going to take Joshua from you."

I snorted, ignoring the pain in my heart at my brother's words. "He's not my kid, Nate."

"That kid worships the ground you walk on."

"He shouldn't. Look where I am."

"You're with your brother, and you're going home. And you're going to stop making stupid decisions. I think that's a pretty good place to be."

I didn't say anything else, knowing there was nothing to say.

I deserved the looks she gave me, any ounce of hatred she threw my way. I was doing things that weren't good for me, even though I was supposed to be the nice guy.

There was nothing *nice* about me. Part of me had died the day I was shot, the day I had thought would be my last. There was nothing left of me for Dakota or her kid. And she saw that better than anybody. It didn't matter that the others thought there could be something more between us.

There couldn't be.

And tonight's meeting had been the final nail in the coffin of who we were. Too bad it'd taken my blood and her fear to make it happen. I might want Dakota more than my next breath, but wanting was good for nothing. She would never be mine. And the only people that didn't seem to understand that were those outside the two of us.

Because Dakota sure as hell didn't want me.

There wasn't much of me left to want.

Chapter 2

Dakota

"MOM, I CAN'T FIND MY BACKPACK."

I pinched the bridge of my nose and looked over the kitchen island to where my son was on his hands and knees, looking under the couch. Apparently, for a backpack that I knew full well could not fit underneath.

"Joshua Bristol. You know that backpack is not there. It's in your room. The same space I told you to clean."

"But, Mom. I did clean it."

I finished packing up his lunch and then reviewed the rest of my to-do list.

"You put away one toy and got distracted yesterday.

But it was Sunday, and we both said we were allowed to be lazy if we wanted to." After I got home from a ten-hour day at work and he was with his babysitter—I ignored the pang in my heart at that. "However, Joshua, you were supposed to pick up the rest of your toys at least and find your backpack before bed."

If I hadn't been exhausted, doing a hundred things at once and trying to find another babysitter since one of my two previous ones quit, maybe I would have been able to help him.

As it was, I was too tired to focus. And all I wanted to do was go back to bed. However, I had already been up for three hours, working on paperwork for the Boulder Bean and doing a bunch of prep for the rest of the week. Finishing cleaning my house was not high on the to-do list.

"Found it!" my son shouted as he ran back into the living room, and I poured more of my coffee into my thermos, knowing I'd need more at work today.

Thankfully, my staff had a handle on opening and had offered to take care of it for me this morning, even though it was supposed to be my shift. They understood that I was a single mom. And, sometimes, even though I owned the business, my son came first.

No, he *always* came first.

Then the business, then my friends...then me. Sometimes.

I groaned. Crap. My friends were supposed to show up today for a quick lunch. That most likely meant the inevitable end of any free time I might have.

I loved my friends, the pact sisters as one of the guys had called us. They were the other parts of my soul, the ones that kept me propped up and reminded me that I was human, a woman, and allowed to have some semblance of a life.

Only I did not want to meet with them today, for obvious reasons.

"Where was it?" I asked as Joshua came stomping in, his too-big backpack over his little shoulders, making him look far too adorable for his own good.

"On the peg in my bedroom."

I barely resisted rolling my eyes. "You mean where it's supposed to be?" I asked with a singsong tone.

"Maybe," he said, drawing out the word. "Can I have a muffin?" Joshua asked, rising to his tiptoes.

"The muffins are at the café, and you already had your cereal."

"But I'm a growing boy. I need muffins."

"Maybe after school."

"But after school, that's the time for cupcakes. You know, muffins with frosting."

I loved his brain. He was a handful, but he was mine. "That's not exactly how that works. And after school, you will be eating your fruit snacks."

"You call them fruit snacks, but it's just fruit," he mumbled.

I went to my knees in front of him, brushed his hair from his face, and looked down at the little man I loved more than life itself.

He had so much of his father in him sometimes that I had to focus to see what parts were from me. I had to look to see them. In his smile, the way his eyes twinkled just like my dad's had.

I loved this little boy with every ounce of my being.

And though his entrance into the world hadn't exactly gone as planned, his existence in it was everything I needed and more.

I would end the world for him. I would do anything for him.

Sometimes I just wished I didn't always have to do it alone.

I shook off that thought and stood up, kissed the top of his head, and held out my hand.

"Okay, little man. Let's get you to school so I can get to work."

"I'm sorry you couldn't go to work today."

I paused as I looked down at Joshua, frowning. "What do you mean by that?" I asked.

"I know you have to open the shop and do all the baking and the cooking. But you couldn't because you have to take care of me," he told the floor, his head lowered. I went to my knees again, hugging him close.

"Joshua Bristol. You are the best thing in my life. If I want to take the morning off so I can hang out with my best bud, I will."

"But how are you supposed to make money and keep a roof over our heads?" he asked, and I held back a wince.

I had no idea where he had learned that phrase, but at six years old, he was far too precocious for his age.

"My staff can help me, and I *will* be working. You have to go do your job, and I will do mine."

"I miss Miss Nancy."

I held back a grimace. Nancy had been a wonderful babysitter until she ran off with the older married man she had been boinking the entire time. The scandal had rocked our little part of Boulder, Colorado, the small town that was anything *but* small.

Now, I was down one babysitter. While I loved Constance, my other nanny, she was in college and had morning classes all semester. That meant she couldn't come over and help with Joshua's morning preparations, which had been part of Nancy's job.

I would figure it out, find somebody I trusted enough. But until then, my friends were helping me pick up the slack, and I would forever be grateful.

Even Hazel's man, Cross, had helped out a few times. His brothers had, too.

I held back a wince at the thought of his brothers. I liked them. I loved his sister. But one of their brothers? I just wanted to throw something at even the thought of him.

I didn't know what it was about Macon, but he set my teeth on edge.

It didn't help that Joshua had begun clinging to him like a little monkey recently. And Macon seemed to encourage it.

He scowled and growled, but then he became the sweetest man to my baby boy. And if there weren't something off about Macon that made me hold back, maybe I'd appreciate that my child had someone to look up to.

But Joshua didn't have a father, not really. And I wasn't going to let him latch on to the Brady brothers when they weren't constants in his life.

"Are you okay, Mommy?" Joshua asked, his voice low.

I pushed away all thoughts of Macon, fighting, and that growl of his that did things to me that I'd rather not think about.

"Mommy is just fine." I shook it off. "Okay, we better go, little man."

"I'm almost a big man. Look how tall I am." He puffed up his chest, and I held back tears.

How was he already six? And going to school with a backpack that was too big for him and little shoes he constantly grew out of?

Life was running away from me. Though, somehow, I was trying to keep up.

My meeting with my friends later today would not help matters. I was not ready for our lunch date. But I didn't think I had a choice.

I got Joshua off to school, waved at his teachers, and did my best not to speed on my way to the Boulder Bean. I had spent a considerable chunk of my savings and had taken out a loan that I knew I'd probably be paying off for the rest of my life for this café. I had worked at the former iteration of the place when I was a teenager. When the old owners needed to sell but wanted me to change the name to make it mine, I had leaped at the chance.

I had put my literal blood, sweat, and tears into its design, the process, and I loved it. I loved coffee, all kinds, and continually tried to find perfect versions of old favorites. I also dug baking and cooking and was able to do a few of those things every time I opened the doors.

I loved every inch of the Boulder Bean and the fact that it had become a hub for my friends and me. Myra, Paris, Hazel, and I couldn't be more different from each other. But, somehow, we had all met up at the Boulder Bean and became friends.

They didn't look down on me because I didn't have the kind of money Hazel and Myra had. Nor the education the three of them had. But they were my friends, and I never truly felt inferior. That didn't mean I wanted to see them today, however.

"Hey, boss," Jason said from the front of the shop as he handed off a large double shot, double whip mocha with extra chocolate shavings.

My blood began to jitter just thinking about the amount of sugar in that, but I didn't judge.

Sometimes, I needed that boost, too.

The man in the high-end business suit who gave me a sly wink didn't seem to fit the usual mocha with chocolate shavings type, but people and coffee came in all sizes, and I loved trying to match them up.

"Hey there, Jason." I looked around to see if there was anything I could do right away before I went to the back.

"Things are in tip-top shape here. Pop's in the back." Jason grinned at me, his dark eyes dancing with happiness. He'd pulled his black hair back into a braid that went down to the middle of his back today and had a bandage on his inner arm that I knew covered his new ink. All of my employees were allowed to openly wear all of the ink they wanted, but Jason's was still healing. I couldn't wait to see it looking vivid against the light brown of his skin.

Pop was a twenty-five-year-old woman who liked to go by the name Pop and was as cantankerous as an old grandpa set in his ways. It made me laugh most of the time. And she was a great baker, so I went with it.

I did most of the baking at the shop with Pop and Jason in the front, but some days, I didn't have time to do it all myself. Hiring Pop meant I didn't have to come in every morning, especially with my babysitter issues.

Both she and Jason worked for me full-time, though I had a few part-timers that rotated in and out, too. We were situated between two universities, as well as many of the businesses of Boulder, and that meant we had a steady stream of customers.

Boulder was weird. That's what the city was known for. Franchises came and went, especially the big green machine that I attempted not to think about. But Boulder liked its quirky and unique, and the Boulder Bean tried for that.

"Seriously, thanks for opening today," I said, hating that I hadn't been able to be here.

"No worries. It's what we're here for. Though as soon as you can replace Nancy, the better." He winked. I could tell he was annoyed with the woman. Nancy had been a great babysitter. She just liked a married man more than she enjoyed watching my son.

I was not going to harp on that, though, because I would only get cranky, and I didn't have time for that.

I waved at a few of my regulars, made a couple of coffees, then went back to the kitchen to work on baking for the late morning and afternoon crowds.

"Hi, Pop," I said, looking over at the woman with the literal pop of color on her head. Today, she was bright pink with a purple stripe that went through her natural curls. Her two nose rings and Monroe piercing shone brightly against the dark brown of her skin and made me feel like I would never be anywhere near as cool and trendy as her.

I'd had a nose ring all of four days before I sneezed and lost the jewelry down the drain. And while I wanted to add color to my hair, it tended to wash right out after a minute. And I wasn't a fan of bleaching because then the curls got all dry and I ended up with a rat's nest on the top of my head.

"Hey, Dakota. Joshua, okay?"

"He's doing great. Thank you for opening today."

"No prob, Bob."

The idea that my staff cared about my son warmed my heart. It was odd, being a business owner and a single mom. I knew that it was a little too much work, and that I would burn out eventually if I didn't find some balance. But Joshua was loved. And that was all that mattered.

I got back to work, focused on baking and getting things ready for the afternoon, and also worked a little bit up front. The Boulder Bean was busy, and the steady pace let my mind focus on work and not wander to the fact that I still had four loads of laundry to do and that Joshua needed a loving mom who paid attention to him and played with him and made sure he got his chores done.

It also kept me from thinking about meeting with my friends to get over precisely what was blocking me.

"Hey, girl, your friends are here," Jason said from the front, and my shoulders tensed.

"What's with that look?" Pop asked. "You love your friends. They're great. Did they do something wrong? Do I need to beat someone up?" she asked, punching her fist into her palm.

That made me snort, and I shook my head. "No, nothing like that. I just have to face the music."

"Oh!" Pop exclaimed, her eyes wide. "So, today's the day?"

I froze. "What are you talking about?" I asked cautiously.

"Today's the day you have to take your straw and become the next blind datee," Jason said from the door and then ran back to the front of the café when I glared at him.

"How on earth do you guys know about that?" I asked.

"We have ears?" Pop replied, shrugging before going back to her baking.

"You guys know… About the blind date pact." My heart raced at the thought.

Pop sighed, then rested her hands on the counter and gave me a look. "Of course, we do. You guys talk about it often enough, and not in hushed tones. It's not like we *want* to overhear your conversations, but we can."

I winced. "Great."

"Don't be embarrassed. It's cool that you guys are taking care of each other and thinking about your futures. If and when I'm ever ready to date and need to be set up, I might ask you guys for help. Of course, you're running out of Brady brothers, so we might need to shop outside of the Brady pool."

That made me wince. "We are not specifically shopping in the Brady pool to find dates. I'll have you know that I don't think we've set up blind dates with the Brady brothers on purpose at all."

That made Pop laugh, her piercings twinkling under the overhead lights.

"See? The Brady brothers just make their way through. Now, that Macon? Oh, my. He's one that I tip my hat to."

"I thought you said you weren't in the mood to date?" I asked, a little pointedly.

Pop snapped her fingers. "I knew it. So, I guess Myra is for Nate, and Macon is all yours."

I held up my hands, warding off whatever her mind was projecting. "No, no, no. I already have enough matchmaking in my life. There is no need for you to add to it. And Macon is not mine. Out of all the Brady brothers, it's never going to be Macon."

"Ouch. What did he do?"

I thought of his busted lip and bruised knuckles and gritted my teeth. "Nothing. Because it doesn't matter."

"Okay. But I still think something is going on between Nate and Myra."

"Just because I might agree with you there doesn't mean I'm going to entertain the idea of setting up the pact sisters with the Brady brothers."

"I don't think you need to entertain anything if it's already happening," Pop said with a smile.

"Get back to work. I need to meet my friends."

"Good luck. I can't wait to hear about your blind dates."

"Pop."

"What? Hazel ended up on an accidental blind date, Paris ended up on the worst set of blind dates until, somehow, she ended up with Prior—not that I know the whole story there. Regardless, it's going to be amazing to see what happens with you."

I growled as I walked away and stomped to the back booth where my friends were seated. I couldn't help but let my gaze drift to the table near the window where Macon had sat with Nate, all growling and bruised.

I still couldn't believe he had gotten into a fight.

I didn't want to hear anything about it. I didn't want to know more. It only reminded me of Adam.

And I refused to think of him.

Bile filled my throat, and I swallowed before I took a seat in the booth.

"Hello, girls," I said. They grinned at me.

Hazel had pulled her hair back in a bun, looking very professorial with her glasses on the tip of her nose. She was radiant, and I had a feeling she had met up with Cross before she came in.

I noticed a slight hickey on her neck, so...yes, that's exactly what she had done.

Paris wore a suit, looking very businesslike and crisp today. That meant she had not seen Prior earlier. I held back a smile at that.

The Brady boys tended to muss up their women.

Not that I was thinking about being messed up by a Brady. I had standards, after all. Okay, I didn't, I had nothing. I was dusty, vacant. Old and hobbly. But that was fine. That's what I needed.

I didn't know why I had agreed to this whole blind date thing in the first place.

"You said that out loud." Myra smiled daintily over her teacup.

I narrowed my eyes. "No, I didn't," I argued.

Myra just shrugged her small shoulders before setting down her cup. She patted her lips dry with her napkin. Myra was old money, class, and sophistication. She was pretty much everything I wasn't.

Yet I loved her so much. Except right now. At this moment, I wasn't a fan.

"You did say it out loud, but I'm delighted that you're next in these blind date shenanigans. Better you than me."

"You know you're next, though," I replied. "And it's probably going to be worse for you because you're last."

"Or, if we take long enough on you, perhaps we'll forget about the whole thing, and I'll never have to do it."

"Well, now that you've said that, I'm adding it to my planner." Paris pulled a planner out of her bag and began writing things down.

"I thought you were all electronic now?" I asked, frowning.

"I am. But I'm trying this new planner craze that isn't that new anymore. It's basically just scrapbooking but with schedules. I'm trying to lower my stress levels.

And I get to play with stickers and something glorious called washi tape. I'm having fun."

I met the other girls' gazes, and we held back laughter. Paris was uptight and controlling, and planners were right up her alley.

"You do not need to add me to your planner," Myra said stiffly.

Paris just grinned. "I think I do. I'm going to remind myself often, even though I shouldn't need to because we're going to get through this quickly."

I froze. "What do you mean *this*? And why *quick*?"

"I mean, we'll figure out exactly who you need to be with, everything will work out hunky-dory and be all lovey, and then we'll move on to Myra. She's going to be the hard one. You're easy." Paris shrugged.

Affronted, I leaned forward. "I am *not* easy. That's why we decided to do this whole pact thing in the first place."

"No need to get snippy," Paris said.

"You know she's just fucking with you, right?" Hazel sipped her coffee.

My shoulders deflated, and I sighed. "No?"

Paris winced. "I was, nothing about this is easy. We promised we would do it, and we do not go back on promises."

"I'm not ready to date," I said.

"Okay," Hazel replied and held up her hands when

both Myra and Paris opened their mouths to say something.

"Perhaps you're not ready to fall in love and get married or do anything that's past a first date." I opened my mouth to say something. "However, we both know that you need a night out. So, let us give you that."

"You mean with a man?"

"Or a woman," Myra said.

"But with an actual date?" I corrected.

"Yes, an actual date. It can be for fun. Your blind date doesn't have to be your future. However, you do need a night out. And your lovable godmothers are going to be here to help that happen. And to watch Joshua," Hazel added.

"I still need to find another babysitter." I rubbed my temples.

"We'll work on that with you," Paris said. I looked up at her. "It's in my planner," she added with a grin.

That made me laugh. "Well, if it's in your planner, then I guess it's going to happen."

"See? And now that Myra's in my planner, as well, that's going to happen, too."

"I'm through with this conversation," Myra cut in.

I laughed as they continued talking about my upcoming date. My tension eased slightly. Maybe this could work.

Just a night out, no promises, no commitments.

If they understood that I didn't want a future with anyone because I couldn't even think beyond tomorrow, maybe this could work.

I would simply do it and get it over with.

And then it would be Myra's turn.

I smiled, nearly missing the look the three of them gave me. I noticed, but I ignored it. I needed to live in my bubble of sanity. And I truly did not need to think about the future.

Especially with a Brady.

Chapter 3

Macon

I SMELLED LIKE CAT PISS AND DOG SLOBBER, AND I WAS pretty sure I had gerbil droppings somewhere on my body.

Regardless, I was having a pretty good day, all things considered.

I walked into my home, stripping off my clothes in the mudroom. I shook out everything, stuffed it all into the washer, started the load, and walked in my boxer briefs to the living room.

I froze and looked around.

"Wow, I wasn't expecting a show," Paris said from

the couch as she set down the ginormous notebook that looked like one of those planner things my admin loved. "I mean really, Macon. Do you always walk into your house naked?"

"He's not exactly naked." Hazel gazed at my junk.

I resisted the urge to cover myself.

Hazel just shrugged. "Well, those boxer briefs are... brief. But they do sculpt nicely."

"For the love of God, Macon. Please cover yourself."

I looked up at my brother Cross and raised a brow. Cross's gaze wasn't on my nudity, thank God. But it was on the scar on my chest. The healed wound that indicated where I had nearly bled out. Where Cross had put his hands, trying to stop the blood.

I vividly remembered pushing Cross off, telling him to go find Hazel. To save her. I had thought I would die that day.

Cross's gaze moved up to meet mine, and I watched him swallow hard.

I didn't know what else to do, so I put my hands on my hips and sighed. "I didn't see your cars out front. And this is *my* fucking home. I'm doing laundry."

"Yeah, you are," Paris said and then let out a yelp when Prior leaned over and bit her shoulder.

"That is my baby brother. Watch those eyes."

"Oh, I'm watching," Paris purred before she yelped

again. I did *not* want to know what Prior did to her for her to make that sound.

"Here." Nate tossed some sweats and a T-shirt my way. "Please put on some clothing."

Nate's gaze slid over to Myra for a second. I didn't think anyone else had caught it, not even Myra. But I had. I didn't know what was going on between them. Though, honestly, I didn't care right then.

"Where are your cars? How the hell did you get into my home? Why are you here at all? I need to shower. I smell like urine, and I had a long fucking day."

"Go, shower. We'll be out here. We brought snacks." Hazel scooted off the couch and came up to me. She looked like she might hug me. I heard Cross's growl, and she winced. "Thank you for letting us in."

"I *didn't* let you in," I grumbled. "Again. Cars. Did you guys park around the corner so I wouldn't see you? Are you ambushing me about something?"

It wasn't lost on me that somebody from our group wasn't here. Was this an intervention about what Nate had seen?

I glanced over at Nate, who gave a slight shake of the head.

Okay, so this wasn't about the fighting.

At least, not yet.

What *was* it about? And where was Dakota?

And why was I so disappointed that she wasn't here?

"Go, shower. Then get dressed and come back. We need to talk."

I looked at Cross and tensed. "Talk about what? Is everything okay?"

"Maybe go cover your dick, and *then* we'll discuss it," Prior said, covering Paris's eyes as she tried to peek.

That made me laugh. I moved past the others. "I'll be quick. But if this is something I'm going to be angry about, get me a beer."

"I'll get you a beer, but you're not going to be angry. You'll probably like it," Nate teased.

Tension filled me all over again. I quickly showered, not bothering to do anything with my hair or beard, mostly just trying to get the funk off. Then I slid into the sweats and shirt that Nate had given me earlier. They were mine, and I liked them.

I made my way out to the living room again to find everyone speaking at once. They all stopped at the same time, and I knew whatever was being said was about me.

I didn't say anything. Instead, I took the beer from Nate's hand and took a swig, narrowing my eyes at my little brother.

"No, it's fine, that was for you anyway." He went back to the kitchen and got one for himself. One of *my* beers.

"Okay. What is this about?"

"Dakota," Myra said, and both Hazel and Paris

glared at their friend. Worry slid over me, but they didn't look too anxious so I figured she was safe. She had to be.

"Are you just going to blurt it out like that?" Paris asked.

"You're the one who usually blurts," Myra added. "I'm breaking the ice. Tearing off the Band-Aid. We don't have a lot of time here."

I sat down on the fireplace, my forearms resting on my knees as I dangled the beer between my legs. "What about Dakota? Are she and Joshua okay?" I asked.

"She's fine. I mean, she's okay." Hazel sighed, then leaned back into Cross since he was standing behind her chair. "As you know, we're doing that blind date thing."

I tensed all over again. "I'm not going on a date with Dakota. We're not blending our groups more than they already are," I grumbled.

"There's nothing wrong with blending," Paris said.

"That's not what you said before you started dating me," Prior chimed in.

"Stop throwing my words back into my face when it doesn't suit me."

I ignored Paris. "What do you need me to do? Though just because I'm asking doesn't mean I'm going to do it."

Myra leaned forward and spoke up, and I didn't miss that Nate glared the entire time. "I don't know what is between the two of you, but you guys keep grumbling at each other. Dakota needs a night out."

"I'm not dating her," I repeated, growling.

"See? The grumbling. The growling. It just keeps happening." Myra held up her hand as everyone started speaking at once again. "Let me continue."

"Whatever you say, princess." Nate glared.

Myra ignored him. "As I said, she needs a night out. She lost her babysitter."

"Because Nancy left with that guy?" I asked.

"You sure do know a lot about her," Nate said. Then rubbed the back of his head after Cross smacked it.

"Watch it," Cross snarled.

"Thank you," Myra said. "Next time, I'll just hit him myself."

"You could try," Nate snapped.

"Are you sure I'm the one who needs to be told that I growl too much?" I asked. Everybody ignored me.

Figured.

Myra stared at me. "Anyway, Dakota needs time away from the Boulder Bean and the house. And you two need to make friends. I don't know why you're always so grumbly, though that is not my business, other than the fact that it *is* my business."

"That does not make any sense," I replied.

Myra shook her head. "It doesn't have to, because I'm right."

"I like Myra," Prior said, and Paris just laughed.

"I love when she gets all prim and proper. It's fun." Paris looked at me. "We're not asking you to go on a real date. More like dinner. Just out. Where she gets to hang out with humans that aren't asking her to serve them and aren't six years old, asking what their farts smell like."

"Macon isn't six years old, but I wouldn't put that past him." Nate grinned, and I glared at him.

"There are ladies present or I'd hit you for that."

Nate met my gaze, and I knew if I weren't careful, he would comment on the hitting thing and my fight club. So, I didn't push.

"As I was saying," Myra said, sounding a little more annoyed than usual, "it's Dakota's turn for a date. You're going to be it."

"Hold up. No, I'm not. Didn't I just say that? More than once?"

"You did. But, yes, you are," Cross added.

"Traitor," I said.

"Nah," Cross replied. "But I *am* your brother. And you need a night out, too. You guys need to get along. I don't know what's going on, just get rid of the tension, and then we can move past this."

"So, all of you are in on this? Forcing Dakota and me on a date?"

"It's not a real date," Hazel said. I wasn't sure I believed her. "It'll get Dakota out, and then we'll be done. We won't force her out on another date. She just needs some time away, and we all promised that this date wouldn't lead to marriage, babies, or anything serious. Just one night of fun." She narrowed her eyes. "But not *too* much fun. She's still family."

I looked at them and then drank the last of my beer in one big gulp. I set the bottle on the brick and ran my hands over my face.

"You're not going to let me get out of this, are you?"

"No, we aren't," Myra confirmed.

"You could try, but we outnumber you. And we can take you."

I looked at Paris, at her little arms, and realized that she probably could take me. She was maniacal like that.

"If she hates me more at the end of this, it's not my fault."

"Dakota's not going to hate you. She really just needs a night out. And, honestly, I think you do, too." Hazel raised an eyebrow.

I looked up at her and swallowed hard. I could still hear her screaming, even when I tried to block it out. Maybe I did need a night out. And I was sure Dakota needed one.

Besides, I wanted to figure out why she hated me.

"Okay. I'll do it."

I held up my hand as everybody started talking at once. "But no outside interference. This is just friends.

That way, she can stop scolding me about every single thing I do."

"You see? What's with the sniping and the growling? I don't know what's up with you two."

I ignored Myra. "But...then we're done. No more dates." Not that Dakota would agree to more. "No more interfering or whatever the hell is going on here. Just let us be."

"We can try," Hazel said. "But she's our best friend, Macon. We want her happy. If she's happy on her own, then that's great. But she needs a night to enjoy herself, and you two need to be friends."

I wasn't going to touch on that. But I would be a good friend. I could do that.

And maybe I could figure out why she hated me so much.

Chapter 4

Macon

THE NEXT DAY, I PULLED AT MY COLLAR, GRATEFUL THAT I hadn't put on a tie. I still wore a suit jacket, a button-down shirt, and nice slacks.

For some reason, I felt like I should have brought flowers or a corsage or something.

It hadn't been that long since I'd been on a date. But, Jesus, I had never been on a blind date.

Though this wasn't really a blind date, at least not for me, though I would be a surprise to her.

We were meeting at an upscale chophouse; one the girls had said Dakota had always wanted to try. I had been there a couple of times before, mostly with my business partner Jeremy and his wife. Thankfully, Jeremy had never set me up on blind dates, even though his wife wanted to. For those outings, I hadn't minded being the third wheel.

This was something altogether different. I just hoped to hell that Dakota didn't throw her drink in my face when I arrived.

Why was I so nervous? This wasn't a real date. I was simply getting our friends off our backs. This was only to get Dakota out of the house. I didn't think I was the right person for the job, but here we were. Hopefully, if the others realized that this was a bad decision, they would stop bugging.

I rolled my shoulders back, ignored the wandering gazes of two women waiting for their seats, and went up to the podium.

"Brady, party of two?" I asked.

"Let's see, sir. Yes. Your other party is already here. Let me show you the way." The younger man in front of me raked me with his gaze. I ignored that, as well. I knew I looked good in a suit, but maybe it was the glare on my face that made him do a double take. That usually attracted more people than I wanted.

Or perhaps I was just having a weird day.

I saw Dakota by a fountain before the host got there, and I tapped the man on the arm.

"I see her. I'll make my way over. Thank you."

The guy stepped back and nodded. "Have a good night."

I made my way towards Dakota, my gaze on her face, so I knew the moment she saw me.

Her eyes tightened, and she glared before slowly setting down her drink and reaching for her bag. She pushed her chair back and stood, her hand fisting around her small clutch.

"You." She whispered the word, and I was grateful. Thankfully, nobody turned to look at us or wonder what the hell was going on.

I had to swallow my words because I could barely think. She looked gorgeous with her hair in an updo thing with pieces that framed her face. She wore a jumpsuit, all black that tucked in at the hips. It was sleeveless and had a low neckline—so low I wanted to peek just to see. Though I knew that that was one of my more lecherous thoughts. Still, I couldn't help it. I'd always thought Dakota was beautiful. So fucking hot, it was sometimes hard for me to think while around her.

And that was part of the problem when it came to Dakota and me.

"Take a seat, Dakota."

"What are you doing here?" she asked.

I moved to her. I towered over her, though I hoped

like hell I wasn't intimidating her. "Our friends asked me to be here, so…I'm here."

She swallowed hard, and I looked down to see the uncertainty in her gaze.

I reached out and brushed my finger across her shoulder. I hadn't even realized I was going to do it until I made contact, the warmth of her nearly too much for me.

She didn't back away, but she did flinch.

I quickly lowered my hand.

She met my gaze as if searching for something I wasn't sure she'd see. "I'll sit down if you tell me what's going on."

"I promise."

She let out a breath and then lowered to her seat.

I tucked in the chair behind her, doing my best not to touch her before sitting across from her.

"Our friends said that you and I need to be more friendly. I'm here to make sure you don't hate me any longer."

I said the words quickly, and her eyes widened.

"So, you're not here because my date bailed?" she asked, her voice soft.

I held back a curse. It hadn't even occurred to me that her mind would go there. "Of course, not. I'm it. Your date. One that isn't supposed to go anywhere. It's not even really a date." I paused. "And I keep saying the word *date*. I'm sorry."

She shook her head and then reached for her water, chugging half of it. The waiter was there in an instant, refilling the glass and taking my drink order. I looked at Dakota. "Am I staying?" I asked.

She studied my face before giving me a tight nod.

I swallowed hard. "A lager. If you have it."

"Excellent, sir." And then the waiter was off, but my gaze stayed on Dakota.

"I'm sorry I made you think that. I promise that you can text the others. They wanted me to be here so we could stop fighting with each other."

"Are they going to do the same to Nate and Myra then?" she asked, and I snorted.

"I said the exact same thing."

"I can't believe the girls did this. And I can't believe you went along with it."

I shook my head. "It all started with me standing in my underwear in my house, pretty much flashing everybody."

Her eyes widened comically. "What?"

"It's a long story."

"I think that's why you're here."

"To tell you why I was in my underwear? Or for me to ask why you hate me?" I asked, trying not to notice how her cheeks flushed at my words.

"Macon," she sighed. "I don't hate you. We're friends. I guess."

"The last time I saw you, you told me to stay away from you and your son." There, now that the words were out, I couldn't take them back.

I felt her gaze, and she shook her head. "I shouldn't have been so cruel about it. But you scared me, Macon. And I don't like that you got into a fight...whatever. I know it's none of my business, but I need to protect my son."

I worked my jaw for a moment as the waiter came over with my drink and told us about the specials.

"We're going to need a few moments," I said, my gaze still on Dakota's.

"Of course, I'll be back as soon as you need me." The waiter was discreet, and I was grateful.

"Dakota, I would never hurt Joshua."

"Maybe not physically, but he's still a little boy. He latches on to people without thinking of what might happen if and when they walk away."

"You don't have to worry about me or my brothers. I know you and I aren't going to be anything." Her eyes widened, and I hastened to add, "Not that we were ever on that path. Regardless, I'm not going to hurt Joshua." I paused. "Or you. We can find a way to be friends. To maybe figure out why we keep sniping at each other."

"It's just so easy to do." She shrugged.

"That's true," I said, snorting.

"I had a very long day. A very long week, truth be told," Dakota began. "It feels like it's been a long year."

"Tell me about it." I rubbed the scar on my chest without thinking. I hadn't even noticed I did it until I caught Dakota's gaze zeroed in on the action.

I held back a curse.

"I'd ask if it hurts, but I know that not all scars ache. At least not in the ways some might think."

There was more to that statement. "Do I have to go and find someone and hurt them for you?" I asked, not entirely joking.

"I don't want any more violence. Especially not things done in my name."

My hands fisted around my drink. "I see."

She shook her head. "You don't. But, honestly, we don't need to get into that. We can be friends. Maybe it's inevitable. And perhaps I need to get over my misconceptions. But, Macon? I don't want a relationship. Joshua doesn't need a new daddy. I don't need anyone in my life who's going to complicate things."

"I don't need anything like that either. I'm only doing this so our friends get off my back."

"Okay, then." She paused. "Maybe we can enjoy dinner."

Relief slid through me, and I knew I wouldn't push.

We'd eat, we'd engage in small talk, and then we'd move on. That's all tonight could be.

"The scallops sounded pretty good," I said, shrugging.

"I was thinking of the halibut. Now, I want scallops."

"We can always share." I glanced at her.

"Maybe. Just don't think that means anything more than the fact that I can't decide between two dishes. I'm not using it as a ploy or anything."

I laughed. "Sounds like a plan. I promise not to fall in love with you." I blurted the words before I meant to, and her eyes widened for a minute before filling with laughter.

"And I promise never to fall in love with you."

We both laughed, and I couldn't help but wonder why I felt a little disappointed.

I didn't need her to fall in love with me. I didn't want that. Yet I felt like I had just lost out on something. But as she smiled, and we finished our drinks and ate dinner, I got to know a little more about the mysterious woman that seemed to hate me on sight.

I didn't know if this would change anything between us beyond tonight. But for a simple meal, one that neither of us had prepared for, it was calming.

Now, I just had to hope like hell I wouldn't regret that promise.

Even if breaking it wouldn't be good for either of us.

Chapter 5

Dakota

I HUMMED BENEATH MY BREATH AS I ADDED WHIPPED cream to the caramel macchiato before drizzling caramel sauce on top. I slid a biscotti onto a side plate and kept humming as I moved towards the front of the café and the corner booth.

"Here you go! Thank you so much. I hope you enjoy," I said after setting down the man's coffee. I gently placed his biscotti plate next to the cup, along with a napkin.

The man with the chiseled jaw and the bright blue eyes smiled at me.

"Well, thank you very much. Dakota, right?"

I swallowed hard, no longer humming. Fear slid over me at the fact that he knew my name. I shouldn't be scared. After all, this wasn't Adam. Nobody from that time in my life knew where I worked. Nobody could come after me. Not that they cared enough to try.

Why did someone knowing my name give me this feeling?

"Yes, I'm Dakota. How else may I help you?" I asked, hoping my voice wasn't as chilly as it sounded in my head. The light in the man's eyes dimmed, and I had a feeling it was precisely as icy as I thought.

"Just thought I'd say hi. I heard your coworker call you by name earlier. I'm sorry if I startled you."

I shook my head and smiled, relieved that had been why he knew my name. I shouldn't be so jumpy. It wasn't like I had problems with anyone but Adam and his crew. The other girls had had issues. If fear-drenched pain could be called an issue. Maybe that's why I'd reacted how I did.

"I'm sorry. Long day. I hope you enjoy your coffee."

"I'm sure I will. And since I've startled you, I suppose asking you out wouldn't be the best idea."

I froze for a second and then noticed his eyes dim just a bit more. "Oh. Well. I'm sorry. I'm well...you know. Uh." Clearly, I couldn't form words.

He quirked a smile. "Let me guess. Boyfriend? I

should have known you wouldn't be free. I see you in here every time I come in. I love your shop. I'm sorry if I was too forward."

I shook my head and ran my hands down my apron. "Oh. Thank you. I love my shop, too. I hope you love your coffee. I need to go. Thank you again!"

He frowned for a second, and I knew everything I said likely made no sense. I waved and then scurried back to the counter where Jason stood, rolling his eyes.

"Subtle," he said.

"I think I just ran away instead of saying no," I panic-whispered.

"Pretty much. You completely ran away instead of telling the guy you weren't taken." He paused. "Unless you *are* taken. If you are, Pop and I are going to need notes."

His humor allowed my shoulders to relax—marginally. "Stop. I need to get back to baking."

"I thought you were going to work on coffee orders with me."

"I think I need to go hide in the back," I replied honestly.

I may have just lost a customer forever. Or perhaps he was made of sterner stuff. Either the man with the blue eyes would be persistent, or we'd pretend it never happened. I honestly didn't know what would happen.

Or what I wanted.

"Coward," Jason whispered under his breath, but I still scurried away.

I'd go back out to the front and have fun with my favorite customers, but I needed a moment. Pop was in the back, her hands elbow-deep in dough when she looked at me.

"What's that face for?"

I put my hands on my cheeks. "What face?" I asked.

"The slightly embarrassed, *oh my God, what is going on* face?'" She paused. "Is it Macon? Is he here? Are you finally going to tell us what happened on your date?"

"I don't know how that's any of your business," I said primly, doing my best Myra impersonation.

"You mentioned in passing that you went on your blind date last week. With Macon Brady. Yet no details. You growl or blush whenever it comes up in conversation, but you haven't told us anything. And now you walk in here looking all embarrassed and flushed... I only have to wonder if I'll see that very sexy man standing out there and glowering if I pull my hands out of this dough and walk out."

"He's not out there," I grumbled. "And I do not look like that. Whatever it is you said."

"You do look embarrassed. So, what happened? Do I need to punch someone?" She pulled her hands out of the dough and punched her hand into her fist once more.

"First, you don't need to hit anyone. Second, why do you do that? Do you enjoy hitting people?" I didn't have the same fear I did when I thought about Macon getting into fights. And I honestly didn't know what that said about me.

Her piercing twitched. "I've never hit a person in my life. I just like making the motion because I'm tiny, and it makes people laugh." Pop must have heard something in my voice earlier. She lowered her hands, concern on her face.

I sighed. "I'm sorry for acting odd. Or odder than usual. Anyway, I just got hit on by a man with pretty blue eyes and I wasn't expecting the offer. I ran away before I could even answer."

Pop just looked at me and shook her head. "Wow. You sure are popular."

"Stop. That's not even close to being true. I feel like I'm making stupid mistake after stupid mistake. I cannot believe I ran away like that. I've seen that man in that exact booth numerous times. Now, he's probably never going to come back because I shunned him and then ran away like I was scared."

"He might have come back repeatedly because you're a hot piece, but he probably also came because you make some of the best coffee ever. Is he the caramel macchiato guy? The one with the pretty blue eyes and the tight ass in those gray pants?"

I blinked at Pop. "Really? You noticed his ass from way back here?"

"I came out to deliver some pastries to the front. Of course, I noticed Blue Eyes' butt. Who wouldn't notice how he fills those pants?"

"I didn't look at his butt."

Pop blinked at me again. "Really? You must have a thing for Macon if you're not checking out other asses."

I threw up my hands and went back to work. "That is not why I didn't check out Blue Eyes' assets. It's because this is my place of business. I shouldn't ogle and sexually harass my customers."

"That's not how this works."

"Not how what works?" I asked, being obstinate.

"Now you're just being weird and going way off subject. Are you deflecting? You still haven't told me what's going on with you and Macon."

"Macon isn't the subject of this conversation."

"He should be. Every time he's the topic, you make up an excuse and run away."

"I do not."

"You *literally* just ran away from a hot man who asked you out."

"I don't want to date."

"And that's the reason you ran?" she asked.

"Maybe?" I said, cautiously. "I don't know. I wasn't

expecting him to ask me out, and I'm not good at this. I don't date. Ever."

"I know. That's why you did this whole pact thing, right?"

"I feel like that was peer pressure," I evaded.

"Perhaps. The girls are good at making sure you're always part of the team. And know that you're loved."

I pushed back the emotions that rose at that. I loved my friends, and I knew I hadn't gone into this because of peer pressure. I was just scared.

"Get back to work. I'm not going to discuss what may or may not have happened with Macon."

Pop snapped her fingers. "You mean something did happen? Because *may or may not* means it did."

I growled. The sound reminded me of Macon. Damn him. "Nothing happened. He showed up as my blind date because our friends were tired of us fighting and wanted us to have a let's-be-friends date. Now, I'm done and never have to go on a date again."

Pop's expression fell. "Really? That's it?"

"That's it. Nothing more." At least, I thought so. I didn't trust Paris or Myra, though. I'd probably end up on another blind date if I weren't careful. "Macon and I are going to try to be a little friendlier for our group's sake." And I would ignore any tingly feelings that arose when it came to him. "Because if we start fighting with each other again, they will force us into another awkward situation, and I don't need that. As for Blue Eyes? If he shows up again, I'll try not to run." I sighed. "And now, after spending far too much time and energy on this, I need to get back to work."

Pop nodded. "Okay. I can go up front and help Jason if you need some time by yourself."

I winced. "Just until Blue Eyes leaves. Because I *am* embarrassed."

"No problem. We stick together." A pause. "Dakota?"

"Yes, Pop?" I asked cautiously.

"You don't have to date anybody if you don't want to. You don't even have to pretend that you want to. You are welcome to be who you need to be. However," she said before I could add anything, "I like Macon. And I like that you guys are going to be friends. I think you could use a friend." She shrugged before I could say anything, then walked out with a bounce in her step.

I sighed and got to work. I couldn't stand around talking about my feelings or my lack of love life. I got busy finishing Pop's dough, began making brownies, and then did another turn on my pastry for a few tarts. I loved my job. I adored baking, and I craved coffee even more. The Boulder Bean was precisely what I needed. Maybe one day I'd be able to branch out into sand-wiches and the like, but I didn't think so. There were enough of those kinds of places near me. We would only be competing for the same customers. It worked out better if we each had our particular niche.

My phone buzzed, and I looked down and held back a curse.

Constance: *Sorry, bad news. Valerie was just offered another full-time job. She's not going to be able to take Nancy's position. But I'm still on the hunt. I know you are, too.*

"Crap," I mumbled. Constance had been trying to get her friend, Valerie—someone I liked and trusted—to take over Nancy's position. However, it seemed like that wouldn't happen.

I grumbled a bit and then texted back.

Me: *No worries. Thank you so much for trying. We will find someone.*

Constance: *You know it. Our little man is amazing. We will find him the perfect person to work with him. It's just weird timing with the semester.*

I nodded, even though I knew she couldn't see me. "This whole thing just sucks," I mumbled.

"What sucks?" Macon asked from the doorway. I turned, my heart racing, and dropped my phone to the floor.

The sound of it hitting the tile echoed, and I winced. I crouched to pick it up. Unfortunately, Macon did at the same time, and we smashed our heads together. I fell on my butt, and Macon reached out, grabbing for me.

"Fuck. I'm sorry. Are you okay?"

"I'm fine," I said, rubbing my head. I picked up my phone. "The screen didn't shatter, and I think my skull is okay. But...*ow.*"

"I'm sorry, Pop told me to come on back because she figured you were in your office. And then Jason led the way. I didn't mean to scare the crap out of you."

"I wasn't expecting you today." I swallowed hard.

He looked so good in his casual jeans and shirt, his face cleanly shaven—though I missed the beard.

"You shaved," I blurted.

He grinned, his eyes twinkling. "Yeah, I had surgery this morning, and it was interfering with my mask. It's why I don't keep a long beard all the time."

Worry filled me. "Surgery? Is whoever you're working on okay?"

He nodded. "Just a spay. Though I can't say *just* about surgery. Our lovely golden retriever, Riley, made her way through easily and is now home with her parents. She is the most adorable golden in the world, at least according to her five-year-old owner."

That made me smile. "Joshua wants a dog so bad."

"Really?"

I narrowed my eyes at his tone. "You knew that, didn't you?"

He winced as we both stood up, and I slid my phone into the pocket of my apron. I was grateful to put some distance between us since it was hard to think with him around.

"He's mentioned it a couple of times, but only in passing. Not like he was trying to get something from me," he added quickly, and I was grateful.

"He isn't a little schemer, at least not yet. Thankfully. But I don't have time to take care of a dog right now. And while he says he wants a puppy, I know he also wants to go to a pound and find an older dog that needs a home. That comes with its own set of problems. And, frankly, I'm not home enough to entertain a puppy or a dog."

"That makes total sense. Pets are a big responsibility, and I'm glad that you're thinking that far ahead, rather than wanting to make Joshua happy or thinking about cute little puppies. Animals are exhausting. It's why I don't have one of my own," he said.

"I always wondered why you didn't."

Macon shrugged. "Between my family and setting up the practice as I have been for the past couple of years? It didn't make sense for me to have a pet of my own, even though I love them. I wanted to be a vet for a reason. My house is pet-friendly, though, because sometimes I need to take an animal home for the night. But the office has a couple of cats, and even Jeremy's family dog comes in most days. I keep thinking about getting a dog that I can bring in to work, but the timing hasn't been right yet. And then, after the shooting, while I recovered, well...I was kind of glad I didn't have an animal at home."

I froze, and so did he. That was the first time he had mentioned the shooting in front of me. I didn't know if he had with anyone else. I wasn't sure what I should say or if I should just move on.

Macon, however, continued speaking, deciding for me. "Anyway, when and if you're ready for a puppy or an older dog, let me know. I'll help you out."

"Thank you, I appreciate it. I just don't see it happening," I said honestly.

"I get you. When Joshua's older, or even now if you want, you can bring him in. I can show him around and let him meet Jeremy's dog. It'll either make it worse for you—and if so, I'm sorry—or it'll give him his animal interaction."

"I don't know if that will be good for him." I hoped he assumed I was talking about introducing my son to animals and not the idea of him spending more time with Macon. Yet when I looked at his face, I saw the hurt there.

"I'm sorry," I said quickly.

Macon shook his head. "No. I get it." I didn't think he did. *I* didn't. "Anyway, I came back to see what you were up to because we're friends now, right?" he asked, sticking his hands into his pockets.

I nodded, swallowing hard. "We are."

"Then great. Anyway, sorry for crashing your head, and possibly breaking your phone."

"It's okay. I drop the thing more often than not, hence why it has such a thick case."

"I think we have the same one," he added dryly.

Oh, boy. Why did that smile do things to me? There were reasons I pushed him away. I just couldn't think of them right now. "Okay, I need to get back to work."

"So do I. I was just taking my lunch break and figured I'd stop by. Hence why I'm not in scrubs."

"I like the jeans," I blurted. He raised a single brow. "Shut up," I mumbled.

"I didn't say a damn thing," he said and then shook his head. "Anyway, I'm heading out. Jason and Pop shoved me back here, by the way. I didn't just make myself at home."

"Ah, makes much more sense." I laughed.

"Jason's surprisingly strong for a man half my size. Anyway, I should go."

"Right. Say hi to the puppies for me."

"I can do that. I'll see you around."

"Yes. See you." He turned on his heel and left, leaving me standing there like an idiot.

I wasn't good at this. Not good with men—or anyone. This was the second time today I had been left standing around like an idiot. Though I was grateful I hadn't run this time. And this was why I didn't date. The only time I had *ever* been good at dealing with men was with Adam, and that was because he only wanted one thing from me.

Well, I wasn't going to let that happen again.

My phone rang, and I answered without looking. "Hello?" I asked.

"Hello, Miss Bristol. I just wanted to give you a courtesy call to inform you that Mr. Dodson has been released early on account of good behavior. He's on parole, but as his parole is in the city of Boulder, you may see him around. The restraining order is still in effect, but Mr. Dodson is free."

I blinked slowly, bile filling my throat. "How can he be free?" I gasped.

"He served his time."

"Not enough," I snapped.

"Ma'am, he served the time for his offenses. You have the restraining order, so call if you see him anywhere near. But there's nothing else you can do. I'm sorry."

The man kept speaking, and I said a few things, though I wasn't sure what. After, I hung up, my hands shaking as I looked down at my phone.

My son's father was out of prison.

Drugs and beating me hadn't kept him behind bars for long.

Another reason I didn't date. Why I stayed away. I had made a horrible mistake before. My judgment wasn't sound.

And now, I wasn't safe.

My son wasn't safe.

And I didn't know how to protect him.

Chapter 6

Macon

I FINISHED MY EXAMINATION, MY HANDS GENTLY PROBING Rusty's side as my aide helped me keep the cat steady. "Hips feel great."

"Oh, thank God. I'm always worried since he grew so fast. I don't want him to be in pain."

I looked over at the worried mother of three-year-old Rusty before sliding my hand down the cat's back and enjoying the purr. I scratched under his chin, and he leaned into my hand, all happy and healthy despite my prodding a few moments ago.

"Rusty's a big boy, a large Bengal who will get into

everything for a long time to come if we have anything to say about it."

Rusty's owner laughed, wiping a tear from her face.

"It's okay, Miss Thomas. He's going to jump from high places and try to get into things. His legs are a little longer than they should be for his body; it's a genetic quirk. So, when he runs, his back legs sometimes get there before the rest of him. It happens to many cats. He's just going to gallop a little more hilariously for you than your other cats do."

"As long as I'm not a bad mom. I mean, he's my baby."

"I understand how you feel," I said, being candid with her.

After talking with Dakota about not having a pet and spending the week helping other people's animals, I knew it was time to be on the lookout for my next foster or adoption. It had been a while since I'd had a pet of my own. It was time. I thought of a cat and a dog, maybe ones that were already bonded so that I didn't have to deal with constant fighting or territorial issues. I didn't always go for puppies or kittens. I generally went for the older animals that people didn't want. They needed homes, too, and I wanted to be that person for them. As long as they didn't mind hanging out at the vet office, they were the perfect animals for me.

Yeah, it was time. Maybe having an animal would be

good for me. Because coming home to an empty house every night wasn't my favorite thing in the world.

"Okay, I'm going to enter a few more things in the chart for Rusty, and then we'll be all set. It was a great checkup."

"Oh, good. My baby boy got a gold star!" She leaned down, and Rusty butted his head into her chin before reaching up to practically hug her.

I met my aide's gaze, and she just smiled, warmth filling her eyes. The family in front of us were perfect for each other, and I was glad that Miss Thomas had Rusty. And I was really glad that Rusty had Miss Thomas.

I finished the paperwork, said my goodbyes, and then headed to my office, rubbing the back of my neck after I washed my hands. I hadn't slept well the night before. Nightmares again. They weren't as bad as usual, though, so I counted that as a win. But I still needed to get some sleep. I'd had another fight two nights before. Thankfully, my knuckles weren't bruised, but my ribs hurt.

I had gone to see my doctor that morning, grateful that I hadn't broken or bruised anything. I knew the man wasn't happy with me fighting, but he understood that it was just boxing and nothing else.

As long as I didn't hurt my hands, those that helped to heal the animals I loved, I would be fine. I just had to keep reminding myself of that.

"Miss Thomas do okay?" Jeremy asked as he made his way in.

"Yes," I said. "Rusty's doing great."

Jeremy nodded. "He gets into so much, but that's Bengals for you."

"I know. If you see him next before I do, just keep an eye on his hips. I made a note in his chart, but with the way he gets into things, those will likely be what he hurts."

"My thoughts were along those same lines. Thanks for the heads-up." Jeremy met my gaze.

"Everything okay?" I asked, a little worried.

My partner sighed. "Things are good here. Just a long day, I guess."

I studied his face and couldn't tell if I had missed something. "Tell me about it. I'm heading out soon. Family dinner."

"No problem. You stayed late as it is. Thanks."

"Hey, it's our practice. I kind of like our job."

Jeremy studied my face and then nodded. "Good. I was worried for a minute that you didn't."

I frowned. "What the hell does that mean?"

Jeremy stood up from his desk and put his hands in his pockets. "When you got hurt, I was afraid you were going to quit. That you were going to decide not to do this anymore. I know we didn't talk about it, but you're my friend, Macon. Not just my business partner. I might be an asshole most days, but I love you. I just wanted to get that out."

I was so still for a moment that I didn't know what to say. "Thanks. I guess." I let out a sigh. "Really. I'm fine."

"I'm sure you are. Now, go see your family. Tell them hi for me. I have one more appointment today, and then I'm heading home, too."

I gave him a nod and headed out to the front. He had a family at home. I had one, too. They just didn't live with me. I had my brothers and my sister and their families.

The fact that an image of Dakota and Joshua in my house filled my brain worried me. Dakota and I were not dating. We were never going to date. She clearly didn't want me.

I needed to get over whatever the hell I was thinking.

I made my way into the front waiting room and nearly tripped over my feet as Nate stood there, a frown on his face.

"What's wrong?" I asked. Considering how many times members of our family had been hurt recently, and with Arden in and out of hospitals, it wasn't an out-of-the-blue or unreasonable question.

He shook his head. "Everything's good, at least as I know it. I just came in to ask you a question. And see if you would drive me to the family thing."

I frowned, grateful that we were alone. "Did you get

a car service to drive you to my place of business before heading to Prior's? Why didn't you just have them take you there directly?"

"First, it was cheaper to come to you. Second, I wanted to talk about getting a puppy."

I knew Nate didn't often drive because of his headaches, and the fact that my brother was currently rubbing his temple made me want to reach out and help. But Nate knew what meds he needed to take, so I wasn't going to offer to get him anything. If Nate needed help, he would ask. Of all of the Brady family members, he was pretty much the only one who was good at asking for what he needed.

"I'll drive you, no problem. You should've just called. I would have come out to pick you up."

Nate shook his head and then winced. "I know, but I needed to get out of the house. And I wanted to see you at work. And...talk about a puppy."

"You really want a puppy?" I asked, walking off to get my stuff as I listened.

"Yes, and I figured your place of business was a good place to start."

I snorted. "We aren't a shelter, Nate."

"That's true. But you can tell me where to find one."

"So, you want a puppy? Not an older dog?"

"I want one I can grow with."

I snorted. "You may be the baby brother, but you're not a baby."

"Fuck you," he whispered, flipping me off.

I flipped him off right back.

Nate continued. "What I meant is that I want a puppy that can work with me and understand that sometimes I have bad days. I don't know. I always thought about holding a little one and growing up with him or her. And it doesn't have to be a purebred."

"But you don't want a breed that has too much energy and needs extra training you might not be able to handle. Or one that constantly barks at a decibel that will give you worse headaches."

Nate winced again. "True. Maybe getting a dog isn't a good idea."

"No, I think you'd be a great dog parent. We can look into the shelters and see what's going on. Who knows, you might fall in love with a dog that's not a puppy."

"I'm completely open to that. I know that shelters around here are usually filled with pit mixes, right?"

"These days, yes. Which is fucking annoying. We'd have to check with your neighborhood to see if there are any issues with certain breeds. I hate that there could be a problem. Some of the sweetest dogs I've ever met have been pits, but people are assholes. Not dogs."

"You don't have to explain it to me. I get it. And, thanks. Whenever you're free."

"Well, I thought I should get a dog as well. And maybe a cat since it's time. We can look together."

Nate grinned. "That's awesome. Perfect."

"Glad I could make you happy. Now, let's get to Prior's. If we're late, Paris will beat us up."

"It's amazing how strong she is for such a tiny woman," Nate said, and I laughed.

"Pretty much," I replied.

We headed over to Prior's, and I parked behind Paris's car. "Arden, Liam, Hazel, and Cross aren't coming tonight, are they?" I asked. The fact that our family was growing as quickly as it was should be alarming, but I didn't mind. I liked the people my siblings had chosen to anchor their lives to.

"No." Nate got out of the car as I did.

"They had other things planned. We are the only ones heading over."

"What about Myra?" I asked, not saying Dakota's name. I wasn't sure I could without accidentally revealing the things I wasn't all that good at hiding.

"Not sure. Don't know about Dakota, either," Nate said pointedly.

We glared at each other before turning to the house, nearly stomping our way to the front door. Prior opened it before we even got there, and Joshua ran out.

"Macon!" the little boy called out. I went to my knees and hugged the kid tight. I looked over Joshua's head and raised a brow at Prior, who only shrugged.

"Hey there, big man. I didn't know you would be here." I picked him up for a moment until he wiggled down. I was grateful since my body hurt. I had gained back a lot of my muscle mass after the shooting, but I still wasn't in tip-top shape. And while boxing was helping that, it wasn't helping the aches. And since I had pressed Joshua to my bruised side, I knew I was going to pay for it later.

"Mom had to work late, and I still don't have a babysitter. Paris said she'd take care of me and brought me here. Now, we're going to eat, and I get to hang out with you guys. I didn't know you were coming. I'm excited because you're my favorite person, Macon."

I nearly took a step back, shocked, warmth filling me.

"I am right here," Nate complained, roughing up Joshua's hair.

"I like you, too, Nate. But you're not Macon."

"Ouch," Nate said with a laugh.

"Hey, buddy. That's not nice." I held back a chuckle.

"Sorry, I do like you, Nate. I like all of you guys. You're fun, and you let me play sports, and we can talk about farts because we're guys. Mom wouldn't let me talk about farts this morning. I don't know why."

I held back a chuckle, feeling Nate's entire body shake at my side. "We can talk about anything you want, kid."

"I'd watch what you say," Nate muttered. My brother had a point. The last thing I needed was Joshua asking about something I couldn't answer.

Was the kid old enough to ask about the birds and the bees? Did he even like girls at this point? Why did I not remember anything about being six other than trying to wrestle with my brothers while keeping Arden safe because she was the only girl in our family?

"Do you want to help me set the table? Paris said I had to do it, but I still can't reach the glasses."

"I've got you, buddy. Lead the way."

"Yay!" Joshua said and tugged my hand.

I followed the kid into the house, nodding at Prior. "Hey there," I said.

"Hi, glad to see you're finally coming into the house. I know I'm no Joshua, but still. I was feeling a little left out."

I didn't flip him off, but I almost did.

"I'm glad you could come." Paris beamed. I leaned down and kissed her on the cheek, and she got a dazed look on her face. "Well, what was that for?" she asked.

"You're family. And I kind of like you."

"Aw, you say the sweetest things. Now, go help Joshua with those glasses before he breaks them. Although, if you break a couple, I wouldn't mind because…did you see what Prior bought?" she asked, and I full-out belly laughed.

Prior strolled into the room, his brow raised. "I heard that. Just because you don't have taste like I do does not mean you can throw away my shit."

Paris narrowed her eyes. "First, language. Second, did you just say I don't have taste? Because you're about to sleep on your couch if you did."

I shook my head, ignoring their bickering. They loved to squabble. It was like foreplay to them. And there were some things nobody else needed to see.

I helped Joshua set the table, listened as he chatted about his day at school and how he missed Miss Nancy. I wasn't a fan of Nancy since she had left Dakota in the lurch, but I didn't say that. It wasn't my business.

Just as we were setting the food on the table, Dakota showed up, her eyes a little wild, her hair falling out of its braid.

"I'm so sorry I'm late. Today has been a day."

She was jittery, looking over her shoulder, and I wondered what the hell was wrong. I had texted her before to ask her a question, and she had been a bit curt with me. We were trying this whole friendship thing, but perhaps I needed to go a little slower. Or maybe it wasn't about me, and I needed to get over myself.

"It's okay. I'm just glad you're here." Paris took

Dakota's purse and nearly shoved her friend towards the meal.

"Oh, I didn't know there was food. Nate? Macon? It's a family dinner?"

"And you're family," Prior said. "Sit down. Eat something that you don't have to cook."

"I can't. I'm swamped, and there's homework."

"Paris already helped me." Joshua hugged his mom hard. She squeezed him back, closing her eyes. When her shoulders shook as she took a deep breath, I frowned, looking at Nate. He shook his head, and Paris looked even more worried.

"Is something wrong?" I asked, not knowing what I was going to say until it was out there.

Dakota's eyes widened, and she shook her head. "No, everything's fine. Just fine. I guess since homework is done, we can stay. You've been so lovely. Thank you. Not having to plan dinner helps when I'm so behind."

"That's what we're here for," Paris said. "Come on, let's eat."

Joshua sat next to me. Dakota took the chair opposite me so I could see her face. She looked worried. I didn't know what was wrong. There had to be something, but she wasn't saying anything, not even after Paris tried to pry it out of her.

The food was good, ribs with macaroni and cheese and corn on the cob. It was a messy meal, though, and I spent half of it wiping Joshua's face and helping him clean off the table as things fell off his plate.

Dakota kept trying to get up to help, but I waved her off. I could handle this. I had been a little boy, too. I knew how messy this food was.

"I'm glad you're here. We have a few things to discuss," Paris said after we'd sent Joshua off to go wipe his face and wash his hands in the bathroom.

"What?" Dakota asked, her gaze on the hallway where Joshua had gone.

Paris continued. "We—the girls and I, that is—have already figured out who your second date should be with."

My hands fisted on the table, tension riding me. A date? Fuck. I didn't need to be here for this. Dakota didn't want me, not like I wanted her, but that didn't mean I needed to know who she would be dating. I turned to look at Dakota.

Her face had gone pale, and she shook her head. "I thought you said I only had to go on the one?"

"That wasn't a date. That was to get you out of the house. You still need the one that's part of the pact."

"No, I don't. I changed my mind."

Paris looked at her, frowning. "You made a promise. And we love you. What's wrong, Dakota?"

I leaned forward. "Actually," I said, hoping I wasn't

stepping on any toes or being an idiot. "Dakota and I already have plans."

Paris's eyes gleamed, and I felt my brothers' gazes on me. "We're still getting this friend thing right. So, she's mine for now."

I hadn't meant to say that last part, but I met Dakota's gaze when I did, and I saw gratitude. At least, I hoped so.

"Oh, yes. We're still doing the friend thing. I guess I can't continue with the pact for now. Sorry."

Paris narrowed her eyes. "You don't sound sorry. But I like where this is going."

"It's not going anywhere, Paris."

I ignored the hurt Dakota's words caused. That shouldn't hurt as it did.

"Becoming friends is helpful," Paris added.

"Okay," Dakota said, clearly not believing her friend. I didn't either. Paris had an agenda.

"I'm all clean!" Joshua shouted and then slammed the door behind him. It echoed in my brain, and I jumped, knocking over my glass of water and nearly falling out of my chair.

Everybody was silent for a moment before Joshua walked back into the room. I did my best to calm my breathing, to fist my hands on the table, to try to think. But I couldn't. All I could hear was Hazel's scream. Feel the blood pouring out of my chest as I gasped for breath.

Joshua was talking, and Nate said something, but I couldn't hear anything past the ringing in my ears.

Dakota looked at me and then down at her phone. I didn't know what that was about, but I couldn't focus on anything. When she stood abruptly, it sent me nearly over the edge again.

"Okay, Joshua, it's time to go," she said tersely.

Everyone looked between us, and nausea filled me. She was leaving. I had scared the fuck out of her again. And now, she was leaving and taking her son with her. She said her goodbyes, and I wasn't sure if I even said anything back. I hugged Joshua when he came to me, but I barely remembered any of it.

Then she left, practically running out of the house with her kid in her arms.

I just sat there, lost in my memories. In my pain.

I wanted her so fucking much. But I couldn't have her. I wasn't good for her.

And the secrets between us? They weren't going to make anything easier.

They never did.

Chapter 7

Dakota

I TOOK A SIP OF MY WINE AND LOOKED AT THE MAN across the table from me. He had a frown on his face, the little line between his brows prominent.

I didn't see Macon scowl as much as I used to. Or maybe I had been doing my best not to study his face. Something seemed wrong, and perhaps it was what we were doing together tonight. Not that I had any idea *what* we were doing.

"I'm sorry Paris and Myra pushed you into this. We don't have to stay long."

He looked up at me then, blinking as if he hadn't

been paying attention. Well, I knew this wasn't a real date, but I still felt a little stung by the lack of interest. Not that I wanted him to be interested in me, but he could at least pay attention when I was sitting right in front of him.

"No, it's no big deal. Sorry. Just had a long day at work."

I held back a grimace and played with the stem of my wineglass. "We don't have to stay. You're the one who told Paris that we needed to figure out this whole friendship thing. But if you're going to sit there and not want to be here, maybe we should just go home and call it a day."

He stared at me for a minute, his frown deepening. "I'm fine just where I am. Maybe we do need to figure out this friendship thing, though."

"I'm confused," I said honestly.

"Well, so am I," he growled.

"What's wrong?" I asked, feeling as if I'd lost part of the conversation.

"I guess I should be asking you that question. I'm surprised you even came out tonight. Or agreed to anything, what with you being so afraid to be near me."

I shook my head. I had no idea what he was saying. "What do you mean?" I asked.

"You know what I'm talking about."

"No, I don't." I paused. "Macon. We may not always get along, but that's for other reasons."

"Other reasons."

I barely resisted the urge to throw up my hands and growl. "I don't know what I'm saying."

"You sure didn't know what to say when you practically ran out of the room with Joshua after dinner. I know I can sometimes be a bit off-putting, but you didn't need to drag your kid from the house."

"What on earth are you talking about?" I asked, my mouth going dry. I'd left Prior's in a hurry for personal reasons. I hadn't even thought about Macon. What had I done to get him to look at me like that? I didn't like it. It might not remind me of the same pain as when Adam had looked at me, but it still hurt to see.

"I know I'm still dealing with the aftermath of the shooting. I know that I sometimes flinch or act as if I don't know where I am. I'm working through that. I have a damn therapist. But, sometimes, I can't control it. If you need to keep Joshua away because of that? I get it. But at least have the decency to tell me and not make me feel like I'm going to hurt you or your kid. Because I'd never do it. You have to believe me."

I just looked at him, wondering how we could be so wrong all the time.

"That is not why I left. I wasn't even… I was in my head, Macon. I swear it wasn't about you. I didn't even realize you were going through something beyond needing a moment." I sighed and put my face in my cupped hands, trying to take a breath.

"What's wrong?"

"I think I'm the one who should be asking that question. Only I'm afraid I'm too late."

I looked around at the small Greek restaurant we were in, at the food we had picked at but not truly eaten, and knew that this wasn't where I wanted to talk to him.

"Do you want to go for a walk?" I asked suddenly.

He frowned. "Are you sure?"

"I just don't want to talk in here."

He studied my face for a moment before giving me a tight nod. "Okay, we can do that."

I knew that Adam could be around, could be watching, but I was doing my best not to live in fear. Or maybe I was trying to pretend that this wasn't happening. I hadn't seen Adam, but I knew he could jump out of the bushes at any moment, just because he liked to fuck with me. Tonight, however, I wasn't alone. And I would make sure that we walked in a lighted area, and that Joshua was safe—no matter what. He was with Constance and her parents at our home right now. They were all taking care of him tonight, while I did something for myself and went on a non-date with Macon.

Because this wasn't a date, it was just two people trying to understand who they were.

"Okay, I'll get the check, and then we'll talk."

"Good. I think… I think I could use someone to talk to," I said honestly.

He gazed at me, and I didn't know what he saw there. But he got up and found the waiter, and soon, we were ready to go.

He put his hand on the small of my back as we crossed the street to the park with plenty of lighting and people milling about. Not so many that they could over-hear what I was saying, but enough that I didn't feel unsafe or alone.

"Okay, let's talk," he said, and I swallowed hard.

"I did not leave with Joshua because of what happened to you. I swear. If I would've thought for two seconds and truly got my head out of my butt to *focus*, I would've noticed you were in pain, and I would've stayed to try and help."

Macon walked beside me. We didn't hold hands, we didn't touch, but I could feel the heat of him. I had to wonder what I wanted, what I was doing. But my needs weren't essential right now. Figuring out how we could continue talking to each other was.

"I thought that you didn't want Joshua near me because I'm trying to deal with whatever the hell's going on in my mind. I don't lash out. I don't hit anybody. But I sometimes break out into cold sweats, and I get stuck in my head a lot. Back in…that time."

I looked at him then and pressed my lips together before letting out a breath.

"I don't know what it was like that night. I do know that you pushing Cross away to save Hazel probably saved her life. But I hate that you were hurt. And I also hate the idea that you thought I would keep Joshua away from you because of your reactions." He opened his mouth to say something, but I shook my head. We paused under a light, and I looked at him. "I wanted to keep you away from him because you were fighting. That's something that I'm still not okay with, and I need to figure out. But I see the way you are with him. And I don't want to bring men into his life that will just walk away. But you and me? We're trying to be... friends. And with so many of our relationships entwined these days, I don't think the Brady brothers are going to be leaving Joshua's life anytime soon." It was a truth I had been reluctant to admit. I didn't even trust myself these days, but I was trying to do better when it came to my son.

"I don't think we're leaving Joshua's life either." He paused and looked at my face. "And I think that means we're not leaving yours."

"I'm not used to that."

"No?" he asked, his voice soft.

It was time that I told him a little bit about Adam so he understood where I was coming from. Not that I truly comprehended it. "I'm going to tell you something, and I don't want you to get angry."

"We've already talked about the fact that I'm trying to handle my emotions. I'm not going to lash out at whatever you say right now."

"But you're still fighting. And I know that's none of my business, but it worries me. Not for me, but for you," I said quickly.

"I'm still figuring out exactly why I do it. Other than I like it. I don't know if I need it, but I like it."

"But you're being safe?" I asked softly.

"As safe as I can be."

"I'm not sure where I stand on that," I whispered.

"I'm trying to find where I stand, as well." We were both silent for a moment before he spoke again.

"Talk to me," he whispered.

"My ex is out of jail," I blurted, and he stared at me, then leaned forward and cupped my cheek.

I didn't even know if he realized he had done it. I froze, not letting myself lean in to the touch, even though I desperately wanted to. I didn't know what was happening between us, what I wanted, what I should feel. I just knew that I had to push him away so I could breathe. Because I was worried. And because he was… here for me.

I couldn't trust myself. I'd already made that mistake before. I couldn't do it again.

"Your ex." He paused. "Joshua's father?"

I gritted my teeth when he let go. I felt bereft. "I used to call him the sperm donor, but that's cruel, especially around Joshua. But, yes, Adam's the one who got me pregnant."

"And he was in jail," Macon said slowly.

"Your brothers never mentioned any of this?" I asked.

"No, I don't even know if Cross and Prior know anything." He paused. "Or if Myra and Nate talk to each other."

"Let's not go there," I added with a dry laugh, wondering how I could even find humor at all.

"You're right. However, my brothers haven't talked to me about any of this. That is if Hazel and Paris have even spoken to them about your past. I don't believe they would betray your confidence like that."

"Oh." I let out a shaky breath. "That's good."

"He was in jail, then?" he asked again.

"Yes, he's not a good guy." I chuffed a laugh. "That is the least I can say about it. Let's just say he was, likely still is, a horrible person. And I fell into him and didn't realize who he was until it was too late for me to get out. He hurt me," I said quickly.

Macon's gaze narrowed. "That's why when you saw the blood on my knuckles after the fight, you reacted as you did."

"Partly." I wasn't sure if I was ready to dive into my true feelings on that, about how the idea of Macon hurt had sent me into a tailspin. "Adam wasn't a good man when we were together. He still isn't as far as I know. He didn't end up in jail because of hitting me. Or doing whatever else he wanted to with me." Bile filled my mouth at the words, but I didn't want to go into detail. Thankfully, Macon didn't ask.

"Why was he in jail, then?" he asked softly.

"Drugs. They got Adam on possession, yet he didn't have enough on him to get any real time. Joshua's six now, and he's never met his father. I got out when I could, ran away, bleeding and in pain. But I got out. And now, well, Adam is out."

I hadn't meant to say so much, but there was no going back now.

"Are you safe?" Macon asked, looking around me as if Adam could show up at any minute. And, honestly, he could.

Chills broke out over my arms, but I ignored them. I had to. "I don't know. The detective on my case is an asshole and doesn't care. There's a restraining order in place, but a piece of paper isn't going to help me if Adam shows up."

"And you and I are standing out here in the dark right now? What the fuck, Dakota?"

"We're as safe as I can be for now. Adam isn't going

to show up when you're around," I said, and Macon's brows rose.

"Excuse me?" he asked.

"He's a wimp. A coward. He hit me because I was weaker. And I know he likely would've done something to Joshua if he'd had a chance. I got away with my son, and I've kept Joshua safe all this time. But he's afraid. Adam, that is. He was always afraid of those bigger than him. Of those who could hurt him."

"I don't hit others unless I'm in a ring," Macon said. "I'm no danger to you or Joshua."

Oh, he might not be a danger physically, but I knew he was a danger to my heart. But that wasn't something I wanted to get into. I didn't want to think about it.

"All I know is that Adam is out there, and I don't know what I'm going to do if he wants to see Joshua."

"We're not going to let that happen." Macon put his hands on my shoulders.

I wasn't afraid. I even leaned into Macon just slightly, needing his touch.

And hating myself for it.

"I'm not going to live my life in fear, but I'm also going to find a way to make sure that nothing ever happens to my son."

Macon looked at me then and nodded. "I'll help. If you'll let me."

I looked at him, at the way he threw himself into

standing up for his family, for his friends. For Joshua. I looked at the long, lean lines of him, his broad shoulders, thick thighs, everything about him. And found it was hard to breathe. That was the problem when it came to Macon. It was hard to do anything when he was around. That was why I fought so hard to keep him away. Because I wasn't sure I'd say no if and when the time came.

He kept looking at me, and when his gaze moved to my mouth, my lips parted, and I tilted my head back. I was in heels, so I wasn't too much shorter than him. I just had to go to my tiptoes, and he had to lean down a fraction, and then his lips would be on mine.

I closed my eyes, and suddenly he was there, a breath away from me. When his lips pressed against mine, no words were needed. His tongue brushed mine, and I held in a moan, needing this. Wanting this. He kissed with such control, as if he were afraid to let the bough break and allow everything to burst forth.

I didn't blame him because I felt the same.

This was a mistake. I had made so many bad decisions, had so many regrets, but I didn't care.

When my phone rang in my bag, I took a startled step back, nearly tripping on my heels. Macon's hands were on my hips, keeping me steady. And he didn't let go.

I looked up into his eyes, his pupils dark and wide.

He didn't release me even as my gaze moved to his lips, locked on the wetness there. I saw the need in his expression.

My phone trilled again, and I pulled it out of my bag, my hands shaking. Still, Macon kept his hands on me.

"Constance?" I asked, my heart racing. Macon's hands tightened on my hips.

"This is Constance's mother, Shireen," the other woman said. "I'm so sorry, but I'm taking Constance to the hospital right now. We think it could be her appendix. Jeff is with Joshua, of course, but my little girl's going to need her daddy. I'm so sorry to cut your night short."

I was already moving towards the parking lot, Macon on my heels. "No, I'm the one who is sorry. I'm on my way to pick him up. I hope Constance is okay."

"I'm so sorry, Dakota. Thank you."

"Take care of your daughter. I'm on my way. Thank you for everything."

I hung up, my hands shaking as I tried to put my phone back into my purse. Macon took it from me and pulled out my keys.

"I'm driving wherever we're going."

"I'm fine," I said, knowing neither of us was likely going to talk about the kiss. Or maybe that was just me.

"I'm driving. And I'm going to call Prior or Cross to come and pick up your car."

"Why not Nate?" I asked, my brain going in a million different directions, yet sticking on an odd fact.

"Nate's been having more headaches recently. He isn't driving as much."

I didn't ask, knowing it wasn't my business. My mind was too busy as it was. "I can drive on my own, Macon."

"Maybe you can, but you don't need to. We'll take your car because the booster's in the back and frankly, because both my brothers have my car keys."

"Really?" I asked as we made our way to my car, my hands shaking. I knew the fear wasn't about Adam. And I knew that Joshua was safe. Regardless, I still needed to get home.

"We've had to help each other out enough that we all keep a spare set of keys for one another. Same with my sister. It's just what we've always done."

"That's smart. Nobody has my keys." I didn't like how sad that sounded. I did just fine on my own, something I needed to remind myself.

"Make a deal with the pact sisters. Or even one of us. We're here for you."

And then we were in the car, neither of us speaking. My knees shook as we made it back to my house. As soon as we pulled into the garage, I practically jumped out of the car, tension riding me.

I did my best to calm my breathing, but before I could open the door, Macon grabbed me around the hips and pressed me to his front.

"Macon," I whispered frantically. My heart raced, but it wasn't from fear. Though considering what had happened to me in the past, I was surprised I didn't scream.

But this was Macon.

And why that would slow my heart rate and let me find my balance...I didn't know.

"Calm yourself. If you go in there like a momma bear looking for her cub, you're going to freak out Joshua. And I bet you he's already pretty upset after seeing his babysitter get sick. You know that kid loves Constance. He talks about her all the time. Just breathe. Walk into the house like everything's fine. If you do that, you're not going to scare him."

I closed my eyes and let out a breath, my hands shaking. I wanted to cry. I wanted to scream. I wanted to do something. But Macon was right. I let myself lean against him, closed my eyes as I rested my head on his hard chest.

"Thank you," I whispered.

"You're welcome. I need to do that sometimes. Little moments trigger me, and I need to breathe so I don't stress others and make things worse. You've got this. Now, go hug your kid."

"Okay." He'd opened up to me, and I knew that meant something, but I needed to see my son before I let myself dwell on it.

"Let's go inside. Joshua needs you."

I opened the door and walked into my home, doing my best not to weep in relief at the sight of Joshua sitting on the couch, rocking back and forth as Constance's father read to him. My little boy was stressed and likely needed a hug. He was getting attention and being cared for by Constance's father, but *I* needed to hold my son.

"Mom!" Joshua said and leapt off the couch to run to me. I went to my knees and caught him, hugging him fiercely.

"Hey, there, baby boy."

"I'm not a baby," he mumbled, burrowing into my neck. "Constance is sick."

"She is. But now that I'm here, her dad's going to the hospital, and he's going to make sure everything is okay."

"Thank you, Dakota. We'll keep you updated. Bye, buddy." The man rubbed Joshua's head before heading out without another word.

Constance's father was quiet but caring. And I knew he was worried. He would keep us updated. So would Shireen. I was worried about Constance, about what it would mean for babysitting duties and Adam...about

Macon. Yet right then, I could only focus on the child in my arms.

"We've got you, little man," Macon whispered from behind me.

"Macon!" Joshua said as if just realizing that Macon was in the room. He nearly pushed me away to scramble towards the man.

I tried not to feel offended.

"Hi, buddy." Macon picked Joshua up, holding him tight.

"You were with my mom?" Joshua asked, looking over his shoulder at me.

I knew my cheeks had reddened, and I didn't know what to say. Macon and I weren't dating. But we had kissed—I could still taste Macon's mouth on mine.

Macon's eyes darkened for a moment over Joshua's head, and then Macon brought him to the couch.

"I heard you had an eventful night."

"Constance threw up, and she was really sick. Her mom got worried, but then her dad said everything was going to be okay. But I'm still scared."

"I understand," Macon said, and I tried not to take in the tableaux in front of me. Macon looking so large and yet caring with my little boy in his arms.

Joshua had never had a father, and Macon wasn't going to be it. I didn't want to get married. I didn't want a dad for Joshua.

I didn't want that connection.

Only…was I making a mistake?

"I think it's past your bedtime," Macon mentioned, bringing me out of my thoughts.

I checked the clock and winced. "It is, little man."

"But, Mom…" Joshua whined, and I shook my head.

"If I hear any updates, I will let you know. But Constance's family is with her, and it's going to be a long night. You need your sleep so you're all strong and ready to go tomorrow."

"Can Macon tuck me in?" Joshua asked, wrapping his arms around Macon's neck like a little octopus.

I met Macon's gaze, wondering what this feeling was inside me.

Macon gave me a questioning glance, and I nodded. "Of course. He's here. Now let's see how he does with the whole bedtime routine."

"I'll be good, I promise."

"Well, at least he made that promise for someone," I said dryly as Joshua ran off to brush his teeth.

"You sure it's okay?" Macon asked.

No.

"I think Joshua just needs people around right now. It's fine."

"And are we going to talk about what happens tomorrow?" Macon asked.

"Nothing," I whispered.

Nothing happens tomorrow.

"Are we going to talk about what happened *tonight?*" Macon asked.

"I don't know," I whispered honestly. "I just need to make sure my son's okay."

"We can do that. And then we'll figure out what comes next."

With a tight nod, Macon followed my son to help with his bedtime routine, and I wondered just how this had happened.

And what the hell I was going to do about it.

Chapter 8

Macon

SOMETHING SOFT WAS ON TOP OF ME. A WARM WEIGHT
that cuddled closer, and my dick hardened at the move-
ment. This had to be a dream. Because all I wanted to
do was let my hands travel and gently cup her ass, make
it so she spread her legs so I could piston into her as we
both came.

I was warm and sleepy and content.

And not awake.

"Macon." My eyes shot open at the little whispered
sound, and I turned my head to the right to see Joshua
bent over me, his nose an inch from mine.

I didn't startle. I didn't shout. My hands squeezed whoever's hips were above me for a bare instant, and then I remembered where I was.

After I had put Joshua to sleep, I had sat on the couch next to Dakota to make sure she was okay. We had talked, but not much.

We must have fallen asleep, because now she was draped over me, neither of us even needing a blanket given the heat we produced.

And, Jesus Christ. Her son had walked in on us.

Not that we had done anything wrong. But I knew she wouldn't be happy when she woke up.

The fact that I hadn't woken up by being startled, fists swinging, said enough about what I felt for these two —even if I couldn't say or think the words. I would never hurt Dakota and Joshua and thank God my subconscious seemed to understand that.

"Hey there," I whispered, my voice morning-rough.

I knew the moment Dakota woke because she stiffened in my hold, the hands on my chest digging into my flesh.

She knew exactly where she was, but like I had, she probably wondered how the fuck we had gotten here.

"What are you doing? Why is Mommy laying on top of you?" Joshua asked.

"Um, we fell asleep."

"Hey, baby," Dakota said before she scrambled off me.

There wasn't another word for what she did. Dakota pushed at my chest, nearly kneed me in the balls, and almost fell off the couch as she staggered to her feet. She straightened her shirt, pushed her hands through her hair, and blinked.

"I think we fell asleep. I didn't even take out my contacts." Dakota rubbed her eyes. "And we need to get ready for school and work," Dakota added before looking down at her phone. "And, crap, we're running late." She cursed.

I was up in an instant, standing on the other side of Joshua and Dakota. "I need to head to work, too. Sorry about that. I didn't mean to fall asleep."

"I guess we didn't mean for a lot of things to happen."

Something cracked inside of me, and I blinked at her, wondering what she could mean by that.

She bit her lip. "I mean...let's talk later?"

Joshua bounced in front of his mom. "What about Macon? Doesn't he need coffee like you? And breakfast. We need to make sure he gets breakfast."

I looked at the two of them, their little family, and I ached. I wanted to be a part of this. When the hell had that happened? I knew I had a thing for Dakota, a huge one, and I knew I loved this little kid like he was mine, but hell. How could I want this? I shouldn't.

"Maybe some other time," I said, looking down at Joshua but knowing my words were for Dakota.

I had just thrown down the gauntlet, at least a little bit. Maybe she'd figure out what she wanted with me.

Because I wanted her.

I remembered that kiss, the need I'd felt, and I wanted more of it.

I didn't remember falling asleep with her in my arms, but waking up with her there?

I wanted more of that.

And I knew it would be complicated. I knew it wouldn't be easy. But I knew what I wanted.

And now I just had to figure out how to get it.

"We need to get ready for the rest of the day." Dakota put her hands on Joshua's shoulders.

"Okay," I replied. "But we're going to talk."

"Yes," she said softly. "We are."

I didn't know what I saw in her expression, but it wasn't denial. It wasn't rejection.

But neither was it acceptance.

What I did see had to count for something, though.

"You're not going to stay for breakfast?" Joshua asked.

I shook my head and then went down to my knee. Joshua came and hugged me tightly, and I inhaled, needing this moment. I wasn't okay. I wasn't completely healed. But for some reason, even though Dakota put me on edge, she and Joshua also settled me.

I didn't know what that meant exactly.

"We'll hang out soon. Now, you should go get ready. I need to head home and do the same."

"And then we can talk about a puppy!" Joshua threw his hands up into the air.

"Joshua Bristol," Dakota snapped, even though there wasn't much anger in her voice.

I held back a wince. "Probably not the best thing to say in the morning before your mother has her coffee. And you shouldn't have mentioned it in front of another person."

"I was just trying," Joshua said, a twinkle in his eye.

"Yeah, and you crashed and burned."

"Fine, no puppy. Ever." He let out a put-upon sigh before running to the back of the house, presumably to get ready for his day.

I held back a laugh and shook my head. "I'm not going to encourage him," I said, and Dakota just ran her hands over her face.

"Macon, about last night—"

"No," I cut in, taking a couple of steps forward.

I checked over my shoulder to make sure that Joshua wasn't around, and then I slowly lowered my lips to hers, holding her chin with my thumb and forefinger as I did.

It was a bare brush of lips, a mere intake of breath, and then I stepped back.

"We're going to talk. You and me. We just fell asleep last night, like normal people do. Like friends. But that kiss in the park? And what I feel right now? I don't think it's only friends."

"I don't know what I want, Macon," she said honestly.

"Neither do I. I already said before that I wasn't going to hurt either of you. I'm not taking that back. So, let's figure this out."

"Macon," she whispered.

"Don't. Let's call it a good morning. I am going to be late for work if I don't leave. And I know you have some babysitter issues to deal with."

"Oh, God," she said into her hands. "I know Constance's parents called last night before we fell asleep, but I still don't know what I'm going to do. She'll need time to heal, and I'm so happy she's going to be okay, but I don't have either of my normal babysitters anymore."

"You know Myra is taking care of it."

"Oh, right. How could I have forgotten Myra?"

"We're both a little discombobulated this morning."

"Tell me about it."

"Myra said she'd be here soon." I looked down at my phone and cursed. "Actually, she should be here any minute. And while I don't want to be here when she shows up, you know Joshua is going to mention it. So no use keeping anything a secret."

"I wasn't planning to keep it a secret, especially since the interrogation wouldn't be worth it." Her eyes widened, and she shook her head before I could speak. "Not that you're not worth it. I don't know. I need coffee. And I can't think. You should go so I can think."

"I can do that. But we're going to talk."

"Okay. I guess so. I'm so confused."

"Go get ready. Myra will help out for the day. And I'm always here if you need me."

"I know you are, Macon. And I think that might be the problem."

And on that note, I walked away, knowing if I stayed, we'd say something we'd likely regret because we weren't ready. I knew she needed some space. And hell, so did I.

Being with Dakota would be like setting up for a ready-made family. I didn't know if I was prepared for that. I liked Dakota, had been falling for her for a while. If I took the next step, it wouldn't just be her and me in the relationship. Joshua would be part of it, but also our friends and family. It wasn't as easy as a single date or our need and desire.

It was so much more.

And that was why we needed a minute.

And yet, all I could think about was how good she

felt in my arms. She tasted like sweet sin, and I wanted more.

It probably wasn't smart for me to dwell on that.

But I didn't care.

I MADE it home and showered quickly and was only ten minutes late for work. My admin gave me a look but didn't say anything. I was never late, was usually *early*, so I was grateful that they didn't hound me because I wasn't sure what I was supposed to say.

"Oh, you're here," Jeremy said when I got back to our office area.

"I am. Sorry. Long night."

He studied my face for a moment before looking down at my hands. "You didn't fight last night?" he said.

"No, I was out with Dakota."

"Finally." Jeremy grinned. "I won't ask for details because we have to work, but...*finally*."

"It's not like that," I began, but then knew that might be a lie. It might be *precisely* that. "We're just...I don't know, figuring things out. Though it's not exactly what you think."

"Okay," he said, drawing out the word. "We have a few changes to the schedule this morning, but we should be able to handle it."

I frowned as I looked down at everything. "What changes?"

"A couple of cancellations and then a few semi-emergencies."

"What emergencies?" I asked, going through the tablet and our schedule.

"It's insect season, and it looks like one of the new puppies is having a poor reaction to some ants. The parents were apologetic and nearly crying over the phone because of a rash, so I know it's not neglectful parenting, it's just the way things are."

I nodded, going through my notes for the day. "Okay, I can handle that. You have a procedure soon, right? The Clemson neuter?"

"That's pretty much my entire day. You get to handle the office visits. I'll handle the part where I feel bad for those dogs."

"You just have a sympathetic reaction," I said, snorting. "But as Bob Barker always said, it controls a population when you take care of this."

Jeremy winced. "You don't have to tell me twice. I still feel bad about it."

"You just feel weird because your wife threatens you with being neutered every time you guys have a little fight."

"Well, if you're going to get personal about it," Jeremy said with a laugh, shaking his head. "By the way,

I hope it works out between you and Dakota. I liked her from the moment I saw her, albeit at a distance."

"You've never actually met her," I added.

"True, but she makes you smile. And growl. And she frustrates you to no end because you have no idea what you feel. It's like Marni and me. It doesn't happen often. But when it does, it's fucking perfect."

"I don't know, Jeremy. It's not that easy."

"Nothing worthwhile ever is."

"I hate that saying," I said.

"I know. That's why I say it often. Because it's true."

"Okay, let's get ready for the day," I growled.

"Let's do that. And then you can tell me exactly how it's going between you and Dakota."

"I thought you said you wouldn't pry," I added dryly.

"I lied."

I shook my head as my friend walked away, laughing.

Jeremy was an asshole most of the time. He and Marni had gone through a rough spot about a year ago, and I'd almost thought we would have to close the practice because of it. I hadn't liked working with him then. He'd made things very difficult.

But now, Jeremy was no longer drinking, and he and Marni had fixed their relationship and even saw a therapist who worked out of the same practice as mine.

They had worked things out and had both apologized to me, and things were going great.

I was happy about that. I had missed the man I'd started this business with, and now we had a practice we loved, and Jeremy was good at what he did. I just needed to figure out *my* personal life.

And, apparently, decide if Dakota would be part of that.

I WAS EXHAUSTED by the end of the day. I knew it was because I hadn't gotten enough sleep the night before.

I might not have noticed when I passed out with Dakota, but it had been late enough that I knew I didn't get enough sleep.

I made it home after work, my neck aching, and my phone quiet. Dakota hadn't even messaged. We sometimes texted, more often than not recently because we were trying this whole friend thing. But I figured I'd scared her away a bit today. Now I would have to figure out what to do about it.

Someone slammed a car door as I got out and headed into my house. I froze, my body breaking out in a cold sweat.

I fisted my hands at my sides, took two deep breaths, and made my way into the house, practically falling to my feet. I pulled out my phone and found my therapist's number.

"Macon. How can I help?"

"I need to talk."

"I'm here. I'm listening."

I didn't say anything for a while, bile filling my mouth.

Then I spoke, just to find my words. To find a way to breathe and make it through this. Maybe Dakota was right, and this wouldn't work. Perhaps I would hurt them in the end. I wasn't together enough to figure out my shit. I didn't need to involve anyone else.

The idea that I might walk away hurt. Only, I might need to.

Dakota had her own problems to worry about, and I didn't want to make it worse.

As I looked down at my fisted hands, at the pallor of my skin, I knew I might be dangerous to her life.

Even if neither of us planned on it.

Chapter 9

Dakota

"I am craving a white mocha with strawberry drizzle," Pop said from my side as she put her hands on the small of her back and stretched.

My stomach rumbled, and I grinned. "You know, I don't work with strawberry in coffee often. It doesn't always work out."

"You're right, but I think it could if we make it sweet enough."

"Just like a raspberry white chocolate mocha?" I asked, my mouth watering.

Pop moaned. "Oh good, now I want that, too."

"I guess if we add enough sugar, we don't need to worry about the taste of the coffee?" I asked dryly, and Pop just snorted.

"Oh, yeah, I could see you not caring about the taste of the coffee. That's so you."

"You've caught me. I think we can make something special, but we're not going to sell that treat in the large size."

"The amount of sugar that'll be in a drink like that? Not very responsible," Pop said.

"We can always pair it with the strawberry tarts. I've been in the mood to play with more pastry."

"I love this place."

I paused and looked over at Pop. "I know you do. But thanks for saying it."

"No, really," Pop said again. "You never let anything get stale. And not just the food," she added with a laugh, and I rolled my eyes. "You always have a plan in mind, and you try out new things. Plus, you work with the seasons. You love this place, and it shows."

"You just made my day. Thank you, honey."

"Thank me? I think I should be the one thanking you. I get to work for a boss that's not an asshole, that lets me work on my own time, and allows me to create. I'm not stuck to a corporate menu."

We both shuddered at the thought but grinned.

"Anyway, how was your night? Have you found someone to replace Nancy and Constance?"

I closed my eyes and groaned. Jason was up front, taking care of any after-lunch-crowd customers. But Pop and I were in the back, getting ready for the next surge of people and whatever we could get done early for the next day.

"No," I said, sighing. "It's getting ridiculous at this point. Everyone that I can trust just can't fit me in. And the process for finding someone new or working with an agency just isn't going to work."

"But Myra is helping, right?"

I nodded, guilt filling me at the thought.

"She is. She's been a lifesaver. Everybody has."

"Do not feel guilty about that," Pop snarled.

"How do you know I feel guilty?" I asked, my voice going a little high-pitched.

"I know you," Pop replied. "You feel guilty over the fact that you need to rely on your friends. Those that offer to help you time after time. People who love you, which you never want to lean on. And now you're forced into it, and you feel that."

"I don't like that you can read me so well," I said wryly.

"You don't need to like it. All that matters is that I know all."

That made me laugh. "Whatever you say, Pop."

"Well, I am brilliant, so you should listen to what I say."

"And what are you saying?" I asked, sighing.

"That it's okay to rely on others. It's all right to need them just as they do you. Your friends love you. *I love you.* And I know Jason does, too."

"Pop," I said, my eyes stinging.

"No. There's no crying in baking. Or baseball. Though I think both of those are lies. Regardless, we're just going to pretend."

"Pop," I repeated.

"No, no crying with me. I'm just saying that you are a wonderful boss, a great friend, and you would do anything to help those you care about. So, let them do the same for you."

"My friends have jobs. They have lives. And I need to find a daycare or something so I can continue to work, to provide. I just—I don't think I can do it all."

"And that's the crux of it, isn't it?" Pop asked softly.

"Maybe. I hate this. I hate that Constance is sick, and even when she gets back up to full strength, I still don't have Nancy's replacement."

"You need both. We need to find you something else. But until then, Myra works from home most days. Which means, she can handle a lot of it."

"Have the girls been talking to you?" I asked, narrowing my eyes.

"Perhaps."

"And did they ask you to talk to me?"

"Maybe."

"Pop."

"What? We care about you. We hate that you're stressed out. And I'll have you know that a very growly man also came in to ask me to make sure I contact him if you need anything but are too stubborn to say it."

I froze. "Macon did what?" I snapped.

"Ha. I didn't even say his name, and you knew who I was talking about."

I flushed. "Pop."

"I'm just saying, he seems like a nice guy."

"He is. But we're just friends. So, no getting that look on your face."

"Whatever you say," she said primly, and I sighed again.

"You are exhausting." I shook my head.

"I know. But that's why you love me."

"No, I think that's why I tolerate you. There's a difference."

She flipped me off, and I rolled my eyes.

"You're such a jerk," I mumbled.

"I am. But you're going to figure this out. You'll find another babysitter or formulate a new plan. And you have a lot of friends to rely on in the meantime. And many of them own their businesses so they can make it work. Plus, soon, Josh will have a thousand afterschool activities because he's growing up and very active, which means you won't have to watch him every hour of every day."

"You *really* do not have children, do you?"

"No. I like being the favorite auntie. I have no plans to procreate."

"Clearly, you do not understand that all those activities mean that someone needs to drive him there. He's already thinking about soccer and swimming. And peewee football. And karate. And art classes. All of those."

"Yikes."

"Yep. And that means money for all those classes, someone to drive him to and from those activities. Someone to make sure that he gets his homework done while he's doing all those fun new things that he might not like after a week. And his schoolwork is just going to increase as he gets older. I need to find a way to work this out. Single moms do it all the time."

"And single moms sometimes have to learn to rely on others," Pop said softly.

"I am. So much more than I used to."

"Okay, then. Now, let's get to making up some recipes for strawberries. My mouth is watering."

"You're a dork." I laughed.

"Hey, um, Dakota?"

I looked over at the man behind us. "What is it, Jason?"

"There's a guy out front asking for you. But I don't recognize him. He may be a customer, but he didn't order anything. He said he wants to see you."

My hands went clammy, and my mouth turned dry. "What does he look like?"

"A white dude with dark hair and a scowl on his face," Jason replied with a shrug. "I'm sorry. He just looks very vanilla."

That could be a thousand people, but it could also be Adam.

I let out a breath and nodded. "Okay, it's probably just a customer wanting to ask something. Or maybe a vendor. I'll deal with it."

Pop gave me a look, and I shook my head before I made my way up to the front.

I knew who it would be as soon as I walked out. "Dakota," Adam said, his voice gruff as if he had run sandpaper along his throat.

"Adam." I swallowed hard.

He had gained some muscle since the last time I'd seen him, but he was still slender and looked wiry. He appeared harder than he had before, though. For a man that'd dealt drugs and handled conflict with his fists more often than not, prison seemed to have hardened him even more, at least in subtle ways.

I could see parts of Joshua in his face, and I hated that.

Loathed that my choices had led to this moment.

I hated that he had helped me create the best and most precious thing in my life—Joshua.

"I see you've done well for yourself," Adam said, his eyes on mine.

"There's a restraining order in place, Adam. You can't be in here."

"I'm just a paying customer. I should be allowed to go wherever the fuck I want."

Jason was at my back, tension strumming through his body. I didn't look back at him. I didn't want Adam's anger directed at anyone else. No, this was just for me. I needed to keep his focus there and not on any of my staff or my friends, or God help me, my son.

Not *our* son.

Adam had nothing to do with Joshua. *Nothing.* And I needed to keep it that way.

"I am the proprietor here. The owner. I have the right to refuse service. And, as it happens, you aren't a customer. You haven't ordered anything. You're loitering. Plus, it's illegal for you to be this close to me."

I knew it was wrong to antagonize him, but I needed him to go.

He smirked. I hated the look on his face. It was

always followed by pain. Emotional or physical. Either way, it hurt. And it was something I could never forget.

"I just wanted to say I'm not done with you yet."

"I'm calling the police," Pop said from behind me, and Adam snorted.

"Whatever the fuck you feel you need to do, go for it. I'm heading out. Don't worry. But remember, I'm going to take what's mine. This place? Couldn't have done it if I hadn't helped you back in the day."

Just his mere presence put an oily sheen on the place I had built. I'd be damned if he cast shadows on it any more than he already had. "You have nothing to do with this."

"I did. I can see you don't understand that. But I know there's something that I *did* have a lot to do with. Something you *know* is mine. Something you're hiding from me."

Chills broke out over my body, but I did my best to ignore him. I had to.

I could not let him find where Joshua was. Joshua was safe at school, and Adam's name was on the Do Not Let Near list. Sadly, it likely wouldn't be enough. I tried my best not to hyperventilate, but he just sneered at me, and I knew he saw my fear. It was so hard to hide it.

"I'll be back. And I look forward to getting to know what I've missed."

He started whistling as he made his way out of my

store, the place that was *mine* and such an integral part of my life. I began to shake, and then Jason was there, holding me, pulling me to the back of the Boulder Bean while Pop was on the phone talking with the police.

"Breathe. Just breathe." Jason sat me down and helped me put my head between my legs.

I tried to push him away.

"I'm fine."

"You might be, but I'm sure as fuck not."

That made me laugh. "Jason. I'm all right."

"Okay. But first, you're going to do this to make me feel better, and then we're going to call your girls. And then we're going to call Macon."

I shot my head up. "You are not calling Macon."

"Why the fuck not?" Pop asked, her phone still in her hand. "The cops are on their way."

"I'm fine."

Pop shook her head. "You need to report what happened. And you *are* going to call Macon."

"I'm not. Macon isn't part of this."

"I think you're wrong," Pop said.

I pushed that away, knowing I needed to see my son before anything else. "I need to pick up Joshua."

"Myra can do it. You need to deal with the cops, and then you're going to meet Joshua at home. Everything will be fine."

"Pop, you need to stop trying to run my life."

"And you need to remember that you're not alone."

And with that, she huffed and headed to the front of the store. My hands still shook.

"I don't need Macon."

Jason shrugged. "Maybe not. But you do need to breathe. And you need to remember that we're here for you."

"I'm fine."

"I know," he said, though I wasn't sure he believed me.

I wasn't even sure I believed myself.

By the time I made sure everything was set up at the store and dealt with the authorities, I was exhausted and just wanted to see my son.

Myra was at the door when I pulled up, and she held up her hand as soon as I made my way to her. "Joshua knows nothing. He just played with paints, and we did his homework. He's having a great day, so you can't go in there and stress him out."

"Myra. I need to see my son."

"I know."

I walked inside but froze when I noticed that Myra wasn't alone. Nate was there, a scowl on his face as he stared at Myra. I blinked.

"Nate?"

"Didn't want her here alone, just in case," Nate said. He came forward, kissed the top of my head, and glanced at Myra. "I'll head out, but you won't be alone for long."

"What do you mean by that?" I asked, but I didn't have time to figure it out. Suddenly, I was on my knees, holding Joshua tightly as he chattered on about his day. I did my best to talk to him and act as if nothing was wrong.

"And then they said we're going to have a class hamster, but some of the moms got upset about it because they didn't want to have to deal with it. So maybe we're not going to get a class pet, but I'm just really excited."

Joshua continued to ramble, and I glanced over to see Nate and Myra whispering fiercely to each other at the door. I looked back at my son.

The hushed voices stopped, and I looked over again, knowing who would be there before I even saw him.

"Macon!" Joshua exclaimed and then ran to him.

Macon picked Joshua up like he weighed nothing and listened as my son repeated his stories about his day. Both Nate and Myra gave me tight nods before heading out, leaving me alone with Macon and Joshua. I had no idea how this had happened. My life was out of control, and I hated it.

Why couldn't everybody just understand that I needed to control my actions? Instead, everybody just kept making decisions for me.

"Hey, buddy, why don't you head to your room and start that tower. I'll head in there in a minute?"

"Okay." Joshua hugged Macon tightly, squeezed my legs as he ran by, and then headed off to his room.

"Don't start," Macon said.

Rage filled me, and I fisted my hands at my sides. "How can I start anything? Everybody's making all the decisions for me. I don't even have a say in my own life."

Macon just shook his head. "We both know that's not the case."

"It sure as hell feels like it," I whispered furiously.

"You're scared, I get that, but we're not taking over. You and me? We're friends. We're figuring things out. But when Myra called? I came. I'll always be here if you need me. Even if we don't figure out what the hell could be between us, I'll be here for you. And that kid."

Tears finally sprang to my eyes, and I put my fist over my mouth, choking back a sob.

Macon cursed under his breath and then pulled me close.

I didn't have long to cry, Joshua could come back into the room at any moment, and I didn't want him to see me like this. He had to see me strong. I couldn't be weak.

"I've got you," Macon whispered.

"You shouldn't have to," I said.

"I've got you," he repeated.

I closed my eyes, letting everything inside me out for the barest of moments, knowing I shouldn't rely on him, but that I could.

I would push him away again when I could breathe. But for now, I'd let him hold me. I'd let myself lean on him.

Even if I knew it was a mistake.

Chapter 10

Macon

I DUCKED UNDER THE FIRST BLOW BUT WASN'T FAST enough to avoid the second. My jaw ached, fiery pain scorching my skin, but I didn't have time to focus on it. Instead, I got in two jabs and an uppercut. After the final blow, the man in front of me was down, taking a deep breath as he rose to his hands and knees, his fists on the mat.

He tapped out, and I let out a breath, knowing if I had taken one more hit, I would have done the same. Jackson and I were equally matched in the ring and usually took turns winning, depending on the day. I maneuvered my equipment and held out my hand, helping the man up.

He took it, spat out his mouthguard, and grinned. "Jesus Christ, you're getting better, Brady."

I spat out mine and snorted.

"Either that, or you're getting worse."

"Ouch. What a bitch," Jackson said as he tore off his gloves and ran his hand over his mohawk. "Seriously, though, you're getting good. You ever think about doing this professionally?"

That made me snort, and I shook my head, both of us going to the side of the ring where our trainers were arguing about something or other. "Not even in the slightest. I don't know if I'm going to continue doing this at all." I said the words quietly, but I knew my trainer heard it. He narrowed his eyes at me, but I shrugged. The guy knew I wasn't in this for the long haul. I was surprised I was still doing it.

If I were honest with myself, I didn't need the adrenaline or the feeling of being in the ring like I used to. I wasn't the same man I was, barely healed from the gunshot wound and stepping into the ring before I was ready.

Though what would take its place? Dakota? No, we'd put that firmly to rest with her taking a step back, even if we were both ignoring what was between us. Maybe I didn't need anything to replace this. I couldn't fight like this forever, putting my body on the line all the time.

"Well, if you want to do it again, I'm in. You don't need go full-out as if you're trying to kill somebody like some of the assholes who walk in here. Maybe you're trying to kill your demons, but fuck, that's why we're all here, right?"

Jackson shook his head, grinned, and then went back to his trainer. Jackson's husband and wife were both behind the ropes, leaning into each other as they rolled their eyes at their husband. The triad had been an integral part of this ring for a while now, and I liked them. Some guys around here were assholes when it came to the union, but Jackson could fight for himself and those he loved, and hell, so could his lovers.

Bob followed me to my locker, while Jackson and his family went to his. "What's this I hear about you quitting?" Bob asked casually, though I knew there was nothing casual about the words.

"We both knew I wasn't going to do this forever," I said, letting him help me with my wrapped hands.

"Well, you come talk to me before you make that decision. You're earning big bucks. You could do more."

"I have a job, Bob. I don't know how much longer I can do this. But it's not going to be for that much longer."

"We'll see," he grumbled before he left me to my

own devices. I stripped out of my shorts and then headed to the showers, knowing I needed a break.

"I can't believe you're fucking doing this," Nate said from the doorway, and I shrugged. I knew he had followed Bob into the locker room, and there was nothing I could do about it.

Nate held up my towel, and I took it as he threw it at me, the end slapping my face.

I turned off the water and then ran the terrycloth over my head and body, glaring at him. "If you wanted a show, you just needed to ask."

"I'm not looking at your dick, asshole."

"Thanks for that. But you didn't have to stay and watch me fight. I'm not being an idiot."

Nate scowled. "We'll agree to disagree on that. I watched the whole thing this time. You're good. You don't go all out and fuck with your safety. And Jackson seems like a decent guy even if I wanted to pull him off you at one point. But I hate that you're doing this at all."

"I'm fine, Nate. I promise." I paused, wrapping the towel around my waist. "Did you Uber here? Need a ride home?"

Nate shook his head. "No, haven't had a headache for a week. I drove."

"You sure that was a good idea?"

"Oh, that's rich, coming from you. Mister I'm going

to go let someone slam their hands into my head repeatedly and see how many concussions I can get."

"Nate," I bit out, cursing at myself for not thinking about why Nate was reacting as he was. The concussion that had ended Nate's career and had sent him on a new path had scared the shit out of all of us. It was the reason Nate had spells where he didn't drive for a while.

And I hadn't even made the connection.

"I only fight people who are smart about what they do. They don't take chances."

Nate shook his head. "You're going to get hurt. And you might be alone when it happens. And because you don't trust us, your family isn't going to be here to help you. What the fuck are you doing, Macon?"

I scowled as I put on my clothes, fisting my hands against the lockers after I did so. "I don't know. I just—it reminds me that I'm here. And it's stupid. I know I don't need this, but some part of me thinks I do. That I'll end up here anyway."

"I'm going to tell the family," Nate said. "I haven't yet because we've had other shit to deal with, but I'm going to tell them, Macon. And you need to figure out what you're going to do. Because if you think I'm upset, what's going to happen when Arden finds out?"

My gaze shot to his. "She's going to kill us."

"No, she's going to kill *you*. She might get upset with

me for not telling her right away. But she'll hurt you. So, don't you fucking dare pretend that this isn't important."

"It is. I know. I need to think."

"Okay. Think. I'm going to head home and have a drink. You need to figure out what the fuck you're going to do. Because what you're doing right now? It's not good."

"I know," I said, feeling defeated.

"Do you?" he asked pointedly and then left me alone.

I didn't even want to be here. I had just shown up because it was almost routine now. And because I needed to think about what I was going to do when it came to Dakota.

Jesus. I had no idea what to do when it came to her.

I stuffed everything into my bag and was near my car when my phone buzzed. I looked down at it and answered right away, my heart in my throat. "Dakota? What's wrong?"

"Why is that the first thing you ask?"

"Dakota?" I asked again.

"I've never called you for something good, have I? Or even texted you for something unrelated to me needing your help."

"Just talk to me." I threw my stuff into the back of my car and then got into the driver's seat, starting the engine. "Do you need me?"

I needed her to need me.

Fuck.

"I'm sorry to call, but I was outside, and I found a cat that looks lethargic and too thin. With four baby kittens."

I froze before my phone went to Bluetooth, and I started my way to her house. "Are they breathing? How big are they?"

"They're breathing and chirping like little babies. Macon, they could fit in the palm of my hand. They're so tiny. I don't know what to do. Do I move them?"

"Keep them where they are for now. I'm on my way."

The relief in her voice made me want to give her the world so she knew she could trust me with anything. "Thank you. Joshua already met the kittens and wants to name them. He's wanted a puppy for so long, but now I think he wants this family. And my God, that's five cats, Macon. And what if they get sick? What if they don't make it?"

"Stop borrowing trouble. We'll figure it out. I'm a vet. It's what I do."

I was nearly at her house after she'd hung up before I realized that I still had blood on my knuckles from where I'd cracked the skin. Well. Jesus. She was just going to have to deal with me as I was. Because it wasn't as if I had the answers she needed, nor was I the man she wanted. I pulled into her driveway, got out of my car, and did my best to run my hands over my jeans.

"Fuck," I mumbled.

Dakota opened the front door, her eyes wide, looking a little scared. "They're meowing and look happy. But I think the mama needs food."

"I'm here. Let me take a look." I pulled my medical bag tighter over my shoulder and stepped closer.

Her gaze met mine, and then she narrowed her eyes. "Did you just get back from a fight?"

I froze at the doorstep and swallowed hard. "Yes. If you need me to go, I will."

"No," she said with a sigh. "It's not my right to tell you what to do. As long as you're safe."

"As safe as possible," I replied, hoping it was true.

"Let's go save those kittens. And my sanity." And then she turned and walked towards the back yard.

I closed and locked the door behind me and followed her to the back patio where Dakota was now kneeling on the ground next to Joshua, worry on her face.

"Macon, can you help?" Joshua asked, his voice small. There was still excitement there, but he was worried.

Dammit, if we lost even one of these kittens or the mama cat, Joshua wouldn't handle it well.

Hell, *I* wouldn't handle it well.

I knelt beside Dakota, ignoring her scent and heat, as I looked at what was in front of me.

The mama cat looked a little thin and run-down, but I hoped it was just exhaustion. It didn't look like there was any bleeding or any apparent wounds, but I would have to do a full checkup here and another in the morning at the clinic. The kittens seemed to be about four weeks old, so they were still too young to be away from their mom.

"There were a couple of storms the past two days. Might have forced the mama to move to another location with the babies," I whispered, nearly mumbling to myself.

"Do you think that's why she looks so tired? That she's cold and sick from it?" Dakota asked.

"I'm not sure, but we're helping her now. Why don't you get whatever towels you don't mind losing to kitten claws, and I'll see what I can do."

"I can get water, too," she said.

"Yes, a shallow bowl she can easily use if you have it. I have some cat food in my bag, ironically." At Dakota's look, I elaborated. "I was feeding a group of feral cats on my block this morning. They're fixed but run free. With the storms I mentioned, they came in for food."

"You're a good person, Macon."

"I'm a vet," I said simply.

She met my gaze before swallowing hard. "I'm glad

you have food. I was going a bit crazy trying to think of what I was allowed to feed her."

"I'm glad I have it with me." I began the checkup as Dakota left, but then Joshua leaned into my side.

"You have a bruise on your face. And some on your hands. Are you okay?" Joshua asked, his voice low.

I knew that Joshua had been afraid when my brother was hurt, as well as Paris and Prior. There had been no shielding him from some of the attacks that had happened in the past. I didn't know what Joshua knew about his father, if anything. So I wasn't going to broach that subject, but I could at least be gentle with my honesty tonight regarding my issues.

"I was boxing," I said honestly. "It's a sport that some adults do. I just forgot to put ice on my cheek like I should have. But it's okay. I'll heal."

"I got you ice," Dakota chimed in, her voice tight. "As well as the blankets and water. And a couple of towels."

"I'll help, Mom," Joshua said, the excitement in his voice coming back.

"Let me finish the exams, and then we'll make some plans," I told him softly, and Joshua nodded. When Dakota didn't correct my use of *we*, I tried not to think about it as a win. She was just protecting her son. I wasn't part of this family. Even if part of me desperately wanted to be.

I finished the exam, made sure the babies were eating, and then hand-fed the mama cat. She was clearly tired but looked to be in better spirits.

"This should be good for the evening. I'll take them into the office tomorrow, and Jeremy and I can figure out what to do."

"You're going to take them away?" Joshua asked, his lower lip quivering.

I met Dakota's gaze, knowing she needed to handle this.

Dakota knelt closer to her son. "They aren't ours, baby. But we can make sure they're safe for now."

"But what happens when they're all better? Are they going to a shelter? One of the ones that kills them?"

I closed my eyes and held back a groan as Dakota gave me a pleading look.

"They aren't going to a shelter," she said. "I don't know what's going to happen, but Macon will help us. You know that we can't take care of five cats. And these are babies. They're going to need lots of attention. But we'll do our best to help."

I cleared my throat. "Your mom's right. They're going to need a lot of love and nurturing."

"I can love."

"I know you can." I ignored how my heart ached at that.

"Are they feral?" Dakota asked, and Joshua's gaze traveled between us.

I shook my head. "No, the mama cat's domesticated. I'll have to check for a chip tomorrow." I looked at Joshua. "If she's chipped, that means she most likely has a home somewhere, and we're going to want to reunite her with her family. She might've gotten lost and scared. But you helped find her and are taking care of her now. That counts for something."

"I don't want her to be sad." Joshua reached out and ran his hand over one of the babies. The momma cat looked at the little boy with such love and trust that I knew this was going to hurt when we split them up.

"Neither do I," I said.

Dakota leaned closer. "Should we bring her inside then since she's domesticated?"

I nodded, noticing that the weather was a bit chilly. "That would be best."

"They can go in my laundry room. I have a little sectioned-off area so the kittens can't get into anything but are still warm and not lost in my couch or something."

I snorted at that. "Okay, we can do that."

It took a little maneuvering, and we were cautious about moving everybody with Joshua helping to hold the kittens. The kid looked like he was in love, and honestly, so did Dakota. Even if she appeared scared as hell about what would happen when she had to say goodbye to these cats. Because I had a feeling she wouldn't be able to keep all five.

"Thank you so much," she said after Joshua had fallen asleep on the floor next to the cats' box.

"You're welcome. I'm always here if you need me."

"As I said before, sometimes I wish I could just call you without needing something."

I tucked her hair behind her ear without thinking and swallowed hard. "You're always welcome to call me. I like the sound of your voice."

She didn't back away. Instead, she let out a sigh and leaned into me. "I wish you wouldn't fight."

"I don't think I'm going to do it for much longer," I replied honestly.

"Good. Because I don't like the bruises on you."

"I told Joshua it was from boxing. Which is the truth. But I don't want to show up around him beat up again."

"Okay," she said. "I should get him to bed."

"I'll help."

"You help with so much, Macon. But you never take anything."

"That's not what friends do," I whispered and kissed the top of her head, not knowing that I was doing so until it was already too late.

I helped tuck Joshua into bed and then went back to looking at the kittens.

I sat against the wall next to them, keeping an eye on them. And then Dakota was at my side, two cups of coffee in her hand.

"It's decaf," she said. "I know decaf is nearly a sin to some coffee drinkers, but sometimes you just need the taste without the boost."

"It makes sense." I took the mug. "Thank you." She sat down next to me, her warm weight solid against my side, and all I wanted to do was sink into her and never let go. But I didn't. I watched the kittens sleep and nuzzle into the mama cat as she cleaned them before falling asleep herself.

I heard Dakota's steady breaths at my side as she fell asleep right along with them.

I knew she had to be exhausted, her days starting earlier than even mine, and her nights filled with Joshua —and now this surprise.

But I didn't wake her. I didn't move her. I pulled an extra blanket over both of us and let myself pretend that this could be real. That it mattered.

And then I fell asleep too, knowing this wasn't reality. It was only a moment in time.

But one I wanted to last forever.

Chapter 11

Dakota

STRONG ARMS WRAPPED AROUND ME AS I SLOWLY PULLED myself from sleep, my brain foggy as I tried to figure out where I was. A mewling sound came from my side, and then there was a rustling and a low voice that wasn't too much of a whisper.

My eyes shot open, and I realized that I was on the floor of the laundry room, practically sprawled on top of Macon while Joshua knelt next to the box where the mama cat and her babies slept.

Though from the adorable little squeaks coming

from the box, the babies weren't sleeping too well and were likely hungry.

I scrambled off, thankful that Joshua's back was to me. Had he seen me sleeping on Macon like that? Again? This was the second time I had woken up clinging to Macon as if he were the last piece of chocolate in the world. And we hadn't even had sex. Yet.

I didn't know why I added that word. Maybe because I wanted him?

No, I couldn't want him. Because if I did, we'd only end up hurting each other in the end. I had too many responsibilities, too many fears to want him. And yet, I knew I did.

I didn't have time to worry about my feelings or needs because my son and five little furry lives needed me. All of me.

"How's mama cat doing?" Macon asked from behind me, and I nearly fell over, not realizing he was awake. I should have. I should have noticed that he was moving, the heat of him behind me, but I had been doing my best to ignore it. Just like I had been doing my best to ignore a lot of things when it came to Macon.

"She's awake, and the babies are eating," Joshua said, his voice hoarse as he rubbed his eyes. "They make really cute sounds when they're eating." He looked over his shoulder at me and smiled that sleepy, dreamy smile that he got when he first woke up. "Did I make those sounds when I ate?" Joshua asked, and I held back a groan. My son was so inquisitive and always asked whatever was on his mind. Even if it wasn't the best question for a six-year-old.

"You still make gobbling noises when you eat your oatmeal in the morning," I told him with a straight face. I just hoped he took the bait and didn't ask me about where babies came from or something.

"I do like oatmeal." Joshua started snorting like a pig, and I held back a laugh.

Macon knelt by the box as he checked on the mama cat and then made sure all the babies were eating okay. "She has some water, but we're going to make sure she has whatever she needs since we don't have a lot of food and litter here. I'll take her and the family into the office today."

"That sounds like a great plan," I said, wondering exactly how I'd found myself in this position.

"Are they going to come back?" Joshua asked.

"We don't know what's going to happen," I answered before Macon had to. Joshua looked up at me, and I did my best to keep my stern mom face on, though not my angry mom face. "Joshua, you know that these babies need someone to take care of them. And we're not home all the time. It's not safe for them to be here."

"I don't want them to go away. I already want to name them. I want them to be mine."

"Buddy, you know we can't have five cats." I wasn't even sure we could handle one, considering I could barely keep up with our lives.

"You're going to split them up? What if they miss their brothers and sisters?"

My heart broke at his words. But thankfully, Macon spoke next, because I had no idea what to say to fix this.

"They'll remember them just like all other siblings do. I don't live in the same house as Nate or any of the other Bradys. But I have them in my mind. And in my heart. Just like these kittens will."

"You get to see them. And eat with them. And play with them. But they won't have that choice if you split them up."

"Sometimes, there are playdates for animals," Macon said, and I couldn't help but stare in wonder as he spoke to my son. It was as if we were a family sitting here.

I had to squash this feeling within me, push it away. It wouldn't be safe to rely on this. I might like it now, or at least like the idea of it, I didn't know what exactly was happening between Macon and me. But I knew I had to be careful. And not just for me. Also for my son.

"Okay, boys, we need to get ready for the day." I blushed as I realized what I'd said, completely ignoring what I had just thought to myself about keeping things at a distance.

Macon just winked at me and grinned. "We do need to get ready for the day. I have to head home, shower, and get changed."

I swallowed hard. "Do you have scrubs in your car? You can use the shower here. That way, you don't have to move the cats more than once." I hadn't even realized I'd said the words until he met my gaze, his eyes going a little dark. Crap. I was not doing well with this distance thing.

"I do. And as long as you're okay with that, I don't mind showering here."

Oh, good, he was going to be naked in my house. And soapy. And washing himself. And…touching himself.

And that was enough of that train of thought. Especially when Macon was giving me a look that said he knew *exactly* where my thoughts had gone.

"Can he use my Avengers soap?" Joshua asked, nearly bouncing on his butt.

"I think he may need adult soap, unless he *wants* to use your Avengers soap, baby."

"I'm not a baby," Joshua said again, and I held back a sigh. No, my son was not a baby anymore. But sometimes I wished I could still hold him in my hands like I could with the kittens currently cuddling into their mom's side.

"Let's get ready for the day. Because you need to go to school, and I am already running late. Again."

Macon frowned and looked down at his watch. "I can drop him off," he said.

I looked up at him, taken aback. "What?" I asked, my voice a little high-pitched.

"I can drop him off. It's no big deal. His school is on my way to the clinic, and if I don't have to go all the way back home, it makes more sense. If that's okay with you."

I could feel Joshua's gaze darting between us, and I couldn't say what I wanted to. That it would be too much. Too much like a family. Instead, I knew I should be grateful that I could lean on him.

I just didn't need it to mean so much.

"That would be good. Very helpful. Pop isn't opening today because she has a dentist appointment, so I need to get in ASAP."

"Okay, then. Let's make this work. You ready to go, Joshua?"

"I still need to get out of my pajamas. And eat break-fast. I want oatmeal." He started oinking again, and I laughed, with Macon shaking his head. It felt...normal.

And I wasn't used to that.

Somehow, the three of us got ready quickly, and I swallowed hard as I gave a spare key to Macon. They were planning to leave in the next twenty minutes or so, but I had to go right away. I didn't know what I was doing, and I felt like I was making all of the wrong choices. But I couldn't go back now. Not that I knew where I would end up.

"Thank you," Macon said, meeting my gaze. "Thank you for trusting me."

"I'll always trust you with his safety, Macon." Unsaid was what I couldn't trust him with. I couldn't hurt him any more than I likely already would.

He leaned closer, and I could smell my shampoo on him. Why was that so damn sexy? "Have fun at work today. Stay safe."

Chills broke out over my arms at the thought of Adam lurking, but Joshua would never be alone today, and I would be in a public place. Adam wouldn't hurt us. At least I didn't think so. I just didn't know what my ex's plans were when it came to Joshua or me.

"Thank you again. Just lock up when you leave and keep my baby safe."

I had to go, but then Macon tucked my hair behind my ear and gazed into my eyes. "I'll take care of him. You take care of yourself."

I wanted him to lean down and kiss me, brush his lips across mine, and tell me everything was going to be okay. And because I wanted that, I moved away, gave him a small smile that didn't reach my eyes, then hugged my son tightly and left. I didn't know why it hurt so much that I wanted how I'd felt this morning to be real —to last. And that I didn't know what else I wanted. But I didn't have time to worry about it or stress.

I needed to open the café with Jason and get ready for the day. Jason was already at the shop since his day started earlier than mine, and we were both quiet as we prepared for customers and set up coffee and pastries.

The morning rush was intense, everybody seeming on edge for some reason, and I hoped it was just the weather change and finals and the like. But I was tired, and my brain was trying to work on a thousand different important things at once. Thankfully, Pop came in right before lunch, and the three of us worked hard from that point on, keeping up with everything.

The lunch rush came and went, and were finally able to take a break before the next swarm of orders. My feet hurt, and all I wanted to do was check on Joshua, even though I knew he was still in school and I shouldn't.

"I'd love a double espresso when you have time." Myra spoke from beside me. I jumped, looking over at her. "I didn't see you come in," I said, a little worried that I hadn't. What else had I missed today?

I looked around as if Adam would jump out from some non-existent bushes or something, but he wasn't here. And the others were on alert, as well. But we had been so busy, what if I had missed a clue or something important?

My heart raced as I tried not to let my thoughts lead me down dangerous paths, but I couldn't help where they went. The school would have called me if something had happened to Joshua. I knew that. I just didn't like that I felt as if I were missing something important or not doing everything I could.

"What's wrong?" Myra asked as I went around the counter, and I hugged her tight.

"Nothing's wrong. I'm glad that you're here, though."

"I'm glad I'm here, as well. I really could use some coffee."

"I'm on it," Pop said.

I smiled over at her. "Thank you, but I've got it. We know somebody's picky."

Myra just rolled her eyes. "Knowing what you like is not being picky. It's smart. And I enjoy Pop's drinks. As well as Jason's. The three of you have made my list."

That made me snort. "And I take it that's a good thing?"

My friend smiled. "I trust you three to make me wonderful concoctions. So, yes, let's call it a good thing. Now, want to tell me what's got that look on your face?"

That made me snort. "Which look, so I can figure out what you mean?"

"I'd say it's worry. And would figure it's about Adam, but perhaps it's something else? Confusion?"

"Myra. This isn't the best place to talk about this."

"Ah, must be Macon, then."

I narrowed my eyes, even though the sound of his name did something to me that I didn't want to admit—even to myself. "I'm still angry at you for sending Macon over yesterday without my knowledge. I can get over the fact that Nate was there without me knowing, considering he came to keep you safe. But you called Macon over. As if he's part of my life no matter what and has a say in what I do."

"First," Myra started, holding up a finger, "Nate was there because he is protective, but not of me. Of you and your son. Nate has nothing to do with me."

I gave her a look but let the lie pass. "Myra, you had no right to contact Macon."

"I had every right," Myra said softly. "Sometimes, you need to share the load. Even when it hurts."

I shook my head. "You don't get to make those kinds of choices for me."

"Your friends are trying to help you. I called Macon because you wouldn't have. He's not trying to take over your life. He's not attempting to take your son from you. But we both know that somebody might."

"Myra," I whispered.

"I know. It hurts. It's horrible. But it's the truth. So, you and me? We're going to figure this out. Along with everybody else. But I called Macon because you wouldn't have, even though you needed to. Somewhere, deep down, you knew you wanted him to be there. And you may hate me for it, but I will always take care of you."

"I hate that you may be right."

"I'm your best friend. I'm always right."

That made me snort. "I don't know what's going on between Macon and me," I whispered.

We were off to the side where nobody could hear us, but I still felt like eyes were on me. Was it Adam? Or was it just the normal busybodies of Boulder, Colorado?

"So, something is definitely going on between you if you don't know what to call it," Myra said.

"You say that, and yet I feel like I should be the one turning it back on you when it comes to another Brady."

Myra raised her chin. "You're welcome to try, but some things are better left unsaid."

"And yet you're trying to get me to talk about Macon."

"What happened last night?" she asked softly.

"How do you know something happened?"

"Because something changed since the last time I saw you. Maybe multiple things."

I sighed and ran my hands over my face. "I found a cat with four kittens, and I called Macon for help."

"Are they okay?" Myra asked, leaning forward. "How old are they?"

"Macon says about four weeks. He took them into the vet this morning."

Myra gave me a look. "This morning?"

"He stayed the night. Again."

"Tell me everything," Myra said.

"It's not as exciting as you might think. He has spent the night at my house twice. With nothing happening either time. But it's like he's meant to be there, and I don't understand how that happened."

"Dakota. It's okay that it's happening."

"It's really not," I whispered. "I don't know what I'm doing."

"Maybe it's all right that you feel like you're floundering. You're in control with so much in your life, perhaps this is the moment when you can allow someone else to step in and shake things up for you. At least when it comes to your heart."

"I don't know if I like the sound of that," I grumbled.

"You may not have a choice."

I sighed and frowned as I looked down at a note under the condiments container on the table.

"What is that?" Myra asked.

"Someone left a note or something. The writing looks familiar…"

Chills broke out over my back as I looked down at the words. I held back a scream.

I'm always here.

Watch your step.

Or I'll take him.

Bile filled my throat, and I looked around the room, but I didn't see anyone.

"It's him. This is his handwriting. He was here. How did he know I'd see it? Because he knew I'd sit here? Or because he figured someone would show me?"

"You're not talking about Macon, are you?"

I shook my head and looked around, nearly spilling Myra's coffee as Pop came over with it.

"What's wrong?" Pop asked, her eyes narrowing.

"Adam was here. He left a note."

"I'm calling the cops."

"I'll call the detective," I said. "He's who I need to contact."

"There's someone else you should call," Myra added.

"The school. Yes, I need to call the school."

"Okay, make that, multiple someones you need to call," Myra said, pulling out her phone. "I'll work on our group text. But you need to call Macon."

I shook my head, even though I knew she was right. Macon would want to know, and for some reason, I felt like he had a right to. Something was changing between us, and maybe it was wrong for me to want him. Perhaps it was wrong for me to lean on him. But all I knew was that having him near soothed me, even as it excited me.

I was probably all wrong about this and making a mistake…yet…I wasn't sure if I cared.

Myra started calling our friends as I called the detective. I hated the man, the way he spoke down to me. But I followed protocol, even though I knew it didn't matter. Because nobody was going to listen to me but my friends and myself. But at least I tried.

I called Joshua's school, and they said he was fine. They even checked on him for me, even if I felt like I was losing my mind.

And then I called Macon.

"Dakota? What's wrong?"

I let out a breath. Again, those were his first words to me. What would happen when I called him simply because I wanted to hear his voice? I was almost afraid I would never allow myself to let that happen.

Or if I did…that we'd run out of time.

"Adam was here, at the café."

He cursed. "Okay, shit. I'm just now seeing the texts from the others." He paused. "Thanks for calling me. Are you okay?"

"I don't know. Joshua's safe. But I just want him home, you know?"

"I'm staying the night."

"Macon," I whispered.

"I need to make sure you're both safe. I know it's irrational, but that's what I need. Will you let me?"

"I think I need it, too," I whispered.

He was silent for so long, I didn't know what he would say next. My heart raced, and I swallowed hard.

"Good. I'll be there. I'll always be there."

I wanted to believe him—knew I needed to.

But I also knew what happened when you trusted someone, and it didn't work out.

I didn't want that to happen again.

Chapter 12

Macon

I WANTED TO HIT SOMEONE. I NEEDED TO *DO* SOMETHING.
Only if I resorted to using my fists, I'd fuck things up
more and scare the hell out of Dakota in the process. So
even though the dreams where I could hear the screams
and feel the pain came on harder and more often,
despite feeling helpless as to what to do about Dakota, I
didn't go to the ring.

And I didn't know when or if I'd be back. I'd ignored
Bob's calls, instead texting back to say I was taking some
time off. Hopefully, he'd believe me and let it go. I didn't

know what the right answer was, but worrying Dakota even more than she already was wasn't it.

"The more you glower over there, the more likely it is Dakota will walk away," Prior said from my side. I frowned and looked over at my brother.

We were at Cross's house, all of us having gathered for dinner to discuss the game plans for keeping Joshua and Dakota safe.

Dakota hadn't been a fan of everybody rallying around her, but somehow, Myra had convinced her that it was the only choice. Adam had left that note two days ago, and nothing had been done. The detective hadn't said much, and Adam was still allowed out on parole, wandering free to terrorize Dakota.

Now, all of my siblings and the pact sisters were at Cross's home, although Arden and Liam were out of town and couldn't join. I'd had to bring the mama cat and her four kittens with me because I couldn't leave them at the vet clinic. They were all healthy, the mama cat was unchipped, and there weren't any flyers or notices in any of the groups that we were part of that matched her description. So far, she was a stray, and nobody was coming to claim her.

I didn't know where she would end up, but I was watching her and the babies for now. And Joshua was in love. Hell, every person in this house had already held a baby, petted the mama cat, and were cooing and falling head over heels.

If I wasn't careful, I would end up with a whole clowder instead of the cat or dog I'd thought to adopt earlier. Though that was if my siblings didn't take one for themselves.

"I'm not glowering," I said after a moment, remembering Nate's snark.

"You're scowling, but that's fine."

"Can I please name her?" Joshua asked, nearly bouncing on his feet.

Dakota glanced at me across the living room and gave me a pleading look.

I cleared my throat. "How about this, Joshua?" I began. "If we still can't find her family by next week, we will pick a name for her because I have a feeling she's going to be staying with me."

Dakota's brows rose, but then Joshua started to do a little dance in the living room, kicking out his feet.

"Now you've gone and done it," Nate muttered.

"I can't let an animal go back out onto the street or into a shelter if I can help. You know this. And it has nothing to do with Dakota."

"That's a lie," Nate muttered, but then he was gone, and the others were kneeling and playing with the kittens or working on dinner.

I went over to Dakota and lowered my head. "Sorry if I went too far."

"No, I want her to be safe, as well. And you are going to be a great cat dad. You already said you were looking for a pet, well now, one's fallen into your lap. Or rather mine, and you're helping me."

"I don't know about all the kittens, but we'll find them homes if I can't handle them."

"I know we will. Or rather *you* will. But I don't think everybody came here to discuss the cats." She gave me a strained smile, and I ran my hand through her hair.

I nodded tightly. "No, we are here to talk about you."

"And that's a great segue," Myra said, coming up to us.

"What kind of segue is needed?" Dakota asked, and I instinctively leaned closer to her so we were side by side.

Myra noticed the action, and I just stared at her. I didn't need her judging me. I did that enough to myself as it was.

"We are here today to ensure that we can make a plan." She glanced over at Joshua, who was playing with the kittens. Hazel cleared her throat.

"Hey, Joshua, will you help me move the box of kittens to the dining room? I want them to be in there while we're eating in case they need anything. I don't know if cats and food go well together, but we're going to make it work." Hazel clapped her hands.

Hopefully, Joshua didn't notice the tension in the room as we all helped them move the cats into the dining area. Before Myra could continue, however, my phone rang, and I looked down at it and cursed.

I nearly declined the man's call, but figured he'd just keep calling, and I'd never get rid of him.

"Just answer it," Nate said, meeting my gaze.

"It's Bob," I replied, as everybody gave me weird looks.

"As I said, just answer. Get it over with."

Everyone looked at me, so I sighed and hit accept. "Bob."

"It's about time you answered me. Are you going to come in for another fight? I have four that need to be scheduled, and you're good with each of them. None of them will be too hard on you, and they're not stupid fighters. I know you don't like the dumbasses."

Bob kept talking, and I pinched the bridge of my nose, aware that everyone was staring at me. Bob wasn't exactly quiet, and I knew they could all hear what he was saying.

Cross's gaze darkened, the same with Prior's.

They glared at Nate, who didn't look surprised, but Dakota came to my side and put her hand on my forearm.

I looked down at her skin on mine and let out a breath. "Bob. It's over. I'm done. Okay?"

"Just like that? You're just going to call it like the fucking pussy you are?"

I must have found a new way to handle most of my rage because his taunts didn't get a rise out of me. "I am. Call Jackson. He fights just like I do. And he still likes it. Dave and William are great, too. But I'm out." I was going to call the guys I liked, however, to tell them I was done, just in case Bob went off on them like he was doing with me. Plus, there were a few others at the gym that I worked with or made sure they got to their cars safely that I wanted to check in with. I couldn't leave everyone high and dry, even if I hadn't really thought about the connections I'd made in my short time there.

"You're going to regret this. You drop me now? You'll never get back into it."

"I'm just fine with that, Bob."

"Whatever. But don't you dare crawl back to me. I won't take you," Bob snapped before ending the call.

I sighed and put my phone back into my pocket. I couldn't help but notice the relief on Dakota's face.

"Thank you," she whispered. I didn't know if it was for herself or for me.

"You want to tell us what the fuck that was about?" Cross asked.

"Cross, Joshua's in the other room," Myra whispered.

Prior snarled. "And Hazel's with him, and she'll make sure he doesn't hear me yell at my fucking brother for being a fucking idiot."

"Fighting?" Cross asked again.

"And it looks like a couple of people in this room knew," Prior snapped. "Were you going to tell us, Nate? Or were you guys just going to keep hiding shit from us? What the hell is going on? And we need to fucking tell Arden, or she's going to be even more hurt than we are. We don't keep fucking secrets in this family. Not anymore."

Everyone started talking at once, and I held up my hands. "Okay, let me just talk this out because this is not why we're here."

"We're here to keep our circle protected," Cross said slowly. "And I guess that means we're going to start with you."

"He just told his trainer or whoever that he's quitting. That should calm you down a little bit." Dakota raised her chin.

I nearly staggered back at her confidence in me. At her tone of defense. I didn't fucking deserve it. But hell, I liked it.

"Why don't we let Macon speak?" Dakota said after

a moment. Then she looked at me. "If that's what you want."

I let out a sigh and nodded. "Looks like I don't have a choice."

"Don't be like that," Cross replied. "You made a choice to not tell us and when you decided to put yourself in danger. Talk to us. That's all we ask."

"After the shooting, I needed an outlet for my rage. I know it's stupid. I knew it was idiotic the whole time. But it's what I wanted to do. And so, I did it. I was as safe as I could be. Except it wasn't completely safe. But I didn't do it every day. I only fought those who fought at my level and played by the rules instead of going against them. Boxing is a sport," I reminded them.

"But you're not a boxer," Nate said softly.

"No, I'm not. I'm a veterinarian who got a bullet in his chest and is still trying to figure shit out. But I'm not going to do it anymore." I looked at Dakota rather than at my family. "I'm not."

"I know you won't. But you still should have told them," Dakota argued, chastising me.

I shrugged. "Maybe. But I'm still figuring out my thoughts. I'm sorry, you guys. I'm not doing it anymore. As Dakota said, that was my trainer. It's not happening again."

"Okay, okay." Paris held up her hands when my brothers started to shout at me. "We don't have time for this," she said. "We're here for Dakota, remember? Yes, Macon, you're an idiot. But we're glad you're safe. And if you do it again, and if Nate holds it back from this family again, then I will have to make this a problem. And you do not want me to be the bad guy here." That made me smile, and Paris just narrowed her eyes at me. "Don't think I'm being funny. I'm not."

I just smiled. "Okay."

Paris flipped me off, and I rolled my eyes. "Now, let's get back to Dakota."

"I don't want to be the center of this," she said.

I shook my head. "I'm sorry, but you are the reason we're here."

"Let's go back to talking about you." She smiled, though it didn't reach her eyes. Without thinking, I brushed her hair back from her face and noticed the others' sidelong glances.

They all wanted to know what the hell was going on between Dakota and me. Well, I wanted to know, too.

But this wasn't the time for that. I had no answers anyway.

And, Jesus, I just wanted to hold her close and tell her that everything was going to be okay, even if I knew it wasn't. At least not yet.

"So, what did the detective say again?" Myra said, looking down at her phone. "I have notes from that day, but I want to hear it once more."

"You took notes?" Nate asked.

Myra glared like the ice queen she pretended to be. "My friend is being stalked. Of course, I took notes. And I'm sure Paris has it in her pretty little planner. If you have a fucking problem with that, Brady, have at it."

"Okay, okay." Dakota put herself between them and held out her hands. "Stop it. Both of you."

"I mean, we can also spend the time talking about what the hell is going on between you two if we want," Prior added.

"Nothing is going on between us," Nate and Myra said simultaneously and in the same cadence.

I just stared at them, and Nate turned away and stalked towards the couch before sitting down and folding his arms over his chest.

Myra leaned back in her chair, crossed her legs, and looked like a prim and proper little princess.

Jesus Christ, I didn't have enough brainpower to deal with all of this.

"Back to Adam," Cross said, his voice low. "Hazel isn't going to keep Joshua away for long, regardless of the cute kittens. Let's make a plan. Because you're one of us, Dakota. We're not letting you get hurt."

"Damn straight", I growled.

Dakota reached out and squeezed my hand, and I wanted to hold on, bask in the warmth, but I didn't.

"The detective said there's nothing he can do. Just like he always says."

"I hate that asshole," I growled.

"Well, so do I. And yet right now, we can't do anything but stay vigilant. The detective said he'd send somebody to talk to Adam, but for now, all we have is hearsay. And a note they may or may not be able to trace to him. I'm not a high priority. My son isn't either."

"You're a fucking high priority to me. Both of you," I added without thinking.

Again, I noticed the glances, but I ignored them.

Myra cleared her throat. "I'm in between projects right now. I can take over most of Nancy's and Constance's duties. Do we think Constance should be alone during this time when she's with Joshua?"

"And you think you *should* be alone with him?" Nate asked.

"I think I have trained in self-defense long enough that I can handle myself."

"And I think nobody should be alone when this guy's out there."

Nate and Myra kept going at it, and finally, I stood up between them as Dakota had earlier.

"If you guys can't handle being in the same room together, you need to go."

"As much as I appreciate all of you," Dakota began,

"fighting with each other isn't helping anything. This is my problem. I can handle it."

I whirled on her. "No, you don't get to back away because they're arguing."

"Joshua is my son. Adam is my mistake. I'll figure it out."

"Fuck, no. You're one of us now. We'll figure this out together."

"Just like you went off to fight with other people? No, you did that alone. You might've walked away, but you're the one who risked your life. You don't get to yell at me if I'm not living up to your standards."

I wanted to growl, but instead, I ran my hands through my hair and started to pace.

"Dakota, a lot of things have happened all at once. And now we're here to make sure that Joshua and you are safe. If that means Nate and Myra have to be alone in a fucking room and not fight while watching your son, that's what's going to happen."

"That's what I was thinking," Nate said snidely.

I glared at him. "You think you can handle that? You think you two can stop sniping at each other and deal with whatever the fuck is going on between you two long enough to keep Joshua safe?"

"Of course, we can." Myra sounded angrier than I've ever heard her before. "Besides, nothing is going on between Nate and me, despite what all of you guys want to romanticize. However, again, I don't need Nate there."

"You damn well do," Nate shouted.

I rubbed my temples, and Dakota fisted her hands at her sides.

She had gone pale, and I cursed.

"Stop yelling. This isn't helping anyone," I said.

"Listen, this is what we're going to do," Paris added, pushing me down to sit next to Dakota on the loveseat. I wrapped my arm around her, pulling her close. She just stiffened in my hold a little but didn't pull away. I counted that as a win. "Myra is going to help Constance, and when Myra is alone without her, then Nate will step in. Both of you work from home. Though I know you can't bring your whole studio with you, Myra. But you said you're between projects. So, until we can formulate another plan, this is what we're going to do. Dakota, I know you hate this, but we are your family. We are your touchstones. We're going to help. And when you're at work, you're not alone. However, if Jason or Pop can't be with you, then one of us will be."

"And you're not staying alone in your house either," I growled.

"Excuse me?" Dakota asked.

"I'm very comfortable on your floor or your couch. Until we get a bead on Adam, consider me your roommate."

"Oh, fuck no," Dakota growled.

"Actually, that might be a good idea," Cross said. "And not just Macon. If Adam is watching your house and knows that there are people constantly in and out, maybe he'll get it out of his head to come near you. Same with your shop. We all work around there, we can come in more often. You're not alone, Dakota."

"I hate this." She rubbed her face. I just held her closer and kissed the top of her head.

"I know. But we're going to fix it. And it's not going to be forever."

"But how long will it be?" she asked.

I didn't have an answer for that. For now, we would work together, be on high alert, and try to figure out what Adam wanted. But until then, we had to stay strong and do what we could. And that meant keeping Dakota and Joshua safe.

Even if she hated it, and even if it hurt my chances for anything more with her.

Chapter 13

Dakota

THERE WERE TIMES IN MY LIFE WHERE I WONDERED HOW I'd ended up in that particular place. Those moments tended to flash through my memory whenever I stood at another crossroads, trying to discover answers to all my many questions.

Like when I ended up pregnant, far too young, and tried to find my way.

When I held Joshua for the first time and wondered how I would do it on my own, yet knew I would fight to the death to ensure that he always knew he was loved.

When my parents left me alone when I was fifteen

and walked away because they were tired of being parents and hadn't wanted to deal with a so-called wayward teen.

The time that I'd had my first drink at sixteen.

And the time I smoked my first bowl with Adam— my first and my last. I hadn't liked the loss of control, but I had been seventeen and thought that's what my boyfriend wanted.

I hadn't realized that by giving up my control, I had given up a part of myself until it was nearly too late.

I remembered the time that I had decided to do something for myself and had earned my associate's degree, right after I got my GED.

And the time I took the job as a barista in the place that was now the Boulder Bean when the former owners had been so sweet to me and had been nearly like grand-parents to Joshua. They had been better than my parents ever were or tried to be. I could remember them vividly, holding my hand when Joshua got his first cold, or making sure I had adequate daycare. They always put his care above all else.

And then there was the time they had left me alone, retiring when Mr. Barker had his heart attack, and we'd nearly lost him.

They moved to Florida to be near their kids and their real grandkids, and I had lost a part of myself when they went. But they had allowed me to start the Boulder Bean.

And that was another moment flashing in my mind.

I had been saving for it, putting away my nickels and dimes, but because of the goodness of their hearts, their business savvy, the loan I had qualified for, and hard work, now this place was mine.

And I was smart with it. Most businesses around here didn't last two years, and we were going on three. We might've had an established base, but in this iteration, we were on three years.

All while Joshua had grown, I had grown, and I had found some of my favorite people in the world.

I had met the girls because of my shop. Had formed a pact to begin my future.

I had met the Bradys.

Everything came together, coalescing into vividly splashed memories across my mind as I worked on cleaning up for the evening.

All of those moments in time were fragments of who I was. When I stood back and wondered how on earth any of it had happened. How could I be here when it felt like fate had been pushing me in another direction, yet somehow, a choice or a mistake or a decision had brought me here.

And now…this was another moment.

Where my past mistakes were coming back to haunt me.

Adam had given me my most precious gift, and yet he was threatening to take it away.

To take Joshua.

To take me?

Maybe to take my business.

I didn't know.

He wanted to take something. Needed to let me know that he thought he still owned me. I didn't know what the answer was. What would be the safest recourse? For now, I had to learn to lean on my friends. And I wasn't doing a very good job of that.

"Hey, there. I need to head home soon," Pop said. "Jason headed out already. Got himself a date with Sam."

I grinned. "Sam is adorable. And I'm so glad that they got up the nerve to ask Jason out."

"It took a lot of time, but I think if they have enough courage to handle the world as it is, they can probably handle Jason."

I snorted at that. "We're all closed up here. I have a few more things to work out in the back, but you can head out if you want."

Pop shook her head, folded her arms over her chest, and leaned against the doorway. "Nope. I don't think so. You know the rules. No one's allowed to be here alone."

"Oh, for fuck's sake," I grumbled.

"You're only saying that because you feel like you're inconveniencing me. I know you're worried about my safety just as much as you're worried about everyone else's—other than yours."

Feeling ashamed, my cheeks reddened. "I just hate the idea that he could come after you because of me."

"You hold on right there. The only reason he would come after me is because of *his* issues. You have nothing to do with it, other than him fixating on you. Don't worry about me. We are going to stay here together. The place is locked, and when you're ready to go, we will head out."

"Actually, if you need to head home, Pop, I can walk you to your car, then stay with Dakota while she finishes up."

Pop and I froze before we spun around on our heels to look at Macon standing in the doorway, his hands up, the keys that I had given him dangling from his fingers.

"Shit, I didn't mean to scare you. I could have sworn you guys heard me. Or even saw me on the cameras."

I looked down at the monitors and did indeed see him. I probably should have noticed him walking closer.

"I've been so stuck in my head that I'm acting like an idiot. I'm one of those people that the viewers scream at in a horror movie to look behind them or to not go down the stairs or lock themselves in the basement. The dumb blonde that gets murdered like in the first scene before they even show the title credits."

Pop burst out laughing, and Macon just gave me a look.

"What?" I asked.

"That was very specific. I feel like you have had this dissertation on horror movies and the way that we portray women in them before."

"It's true," Pop said. "Don't even get me started."

"One day, I'd like to hear it," Macon added. "However, the place is locked, and I'll get you to your car safely, Pop. You can stay right here, Dakota."

"I don't think so," I said. "I have some more work to do, and Joshua is at a sleepover. I can walk you out together, and then come back in."

Macon nodded. "Sounds good. Joshua stopped by here earlier to say goodnight, right?"

I smiled, my heart growing two sizes at the thought. "He was so cute and excited. He can't wait to tell them all about Mama Cat and her babies."

Macon winced. "I think we named her Mama Cat. My grandfather had a cat up in Oregon named Mama Cat, actually. A wild feral that hated me. However, it looks like the new Mama Cat has a name."

I shook my head. "Either that or we'll make something work."

"Oh, you guys are too cute."

I glared at Pop and then grabbed my phone. "Come on. We'll walk you to your car. I have to stay here and finish up the last couple of things that can't be done at home. If I didn't, I would head out for the day with you."

Pop studied my face. "Just stay safe. And I want to hear all about Joshua's sleepover."

"I can't believe my baby boy is big enough for a sleepover," I said, and Macon wrapped his arm around my shoulders and kissed the top of my head.

"Well, he's still going to come running to you for a long while."

"Six just seems too young."

Macon shrugged. "It's with his best friend, and I have a feeling the other boy's mother has already been texting you."

"Every twenty minutes with pictures. They're adorable."

"Make sure you show them to me, too," Pop said.

"I'll forward them to you," I ensured.

We made sure Pop got to her car. After she drove off, Macon took my hand and led me back into the Boulder Bean. We closed the area, made sure it was locked, then went back to my office.

"I hate that you have to be here for this. There are just some things I need to finish here. After that, we do not have to stay. It's got to be boring for you."

Macon shook his head and then pulled out his tablet. "I have a few things I can do here. And you have this nice comfy chair. Don't worry, we'll just work some, and then we'll get something to eat."

"You're going to stay the night?" I asked, swallowing hard.

"You know I want to," he whispered.

"What are we doing?" I asked without thinking.

He set down his tablet on the desk and then stood up, prowling towards me. He put a hand on either side of me on my office chair and leaned forward, his forehead resting against mine, his presence so big, so...Macon.

"What is it you think we're doing?" he asked.

"You can't just ask a question in answer to a question."

"I do believe I have. Now, I suppose I should answer your original one. As to what we're doing? Anything you want. But you know we're not just friends, Dakota. You can lie to yourself, but you can't lie to me."

I swallowed hard, looking up at him. I wanted to reach out and trail my fingers down his chest, but I didn't. Somehow, I resisted. "You know this is a mistake. There's so much going on. We shouldn't. I don't want to hurt you."

He leaned forward just a bit more, his lips close to

mine. "You're not going to hurt me. And I'm not going to hurt you. But, Dakota? I want to fucking kiss you."

"Then kiss me," I whispered.

Suddenly, his lips were on mine, and I was lost.

He kissed me slowly as if learning my mouth, figuring out exactly what I tasted like and absorbing the essence of my touch. He tasted of coffee and warmth. And I wanted more. I craved it.

And then my hands were on his chest, feeling the hardness of him. When my palm moved over the center of his chest, he froze for the barest instant, and I pulled away.

"I'm sorry," I whispered.

"Scar's always going to be there, Dakota. I guess I should get used to you touching it."

"I thought that was my line," I whispered.

He smiled then and reached up to pluck me off the chair.

I let out a gasp, and then my ass was on my desk, his tablet hitting the floor.

"Macon!"

"It's insured. It'll be fine. Probably. I don't give a fuck."

When his mouth crashed into mine, I dug my fingers into his hair, and he squeezed my hips. He slid in between my legs, and I wrapped myself around him, clinging, needing.

"This is insane," I whispered.

"This is a long time coming."

He kept kissing me, trailing his lips down my neck, tugging on my shirt. I did the same for him, and he held up his arms and let me strip him. He had put on a t-shirt after work, and now he was bare to his jeans, the long, lean lines of him intoxicating. His chest was broad, and he had an eight-pack. A freaking eight-pack.

And even though I knew it was wrong, I wanted to picture him in the ring, sweat-slick as he fought and used every single one of his muscles.

Of course, I also wanted to see those muscles being used in other ways, as he hovered over me, sliding inside me.

"What just gave you that look? What were you thinking?" he asked, hesitance in his voice.

I looked up at him, past the scar I knew he thought I was staring at.

"I was thinking about you fucking me after you fought. And I knew it was wrong." I reached out and gently laid my hand over his scar. He twitched, freezing. "Macon, I wasn't thinking about this. Unless you want me to. I was just thinking about you."

He put his hand over mine and squeezed. "I want to see you."

"Then do. And touch me. Because I don't think I can wait any longer."

Who was this woman? I had been on dates before, a couple after Adam. I'd had sex before. I liked it. I used to think I was good at sex.

But this woman? The one who spoke as if she couldn't get enough and said what she wanted?

It didn't feel like me.

But I loved it.

He stripped off my shirt, and then his hands were on my breasts over my bra. I moaned, letting my head fall back.

"You're so beautiful."

"I have stretch marks from Joshua. I'm not a skinny little model. You're all hard and fit. I'm not exactly that."

"You're fucking beautiful, and if you put yourself down one more time, I'm going to toss you over my knee and spank you."

My eyes widened. "Macon Brady. Is that your kink?" I asked with a laugh that wasn't so much full of humor as intrigue. I pressed my thighs tighter around his hips at the thought. I was not into spanking, but the idea of Macon doing it? That, I might need to imagine.

"It's not, but the idea of my hand on that ass of yours? I may have to try."

And then he kissed me again, and my bra was off. He moved to his knees in front of me, my desk low enough that he was able to kiss up my stomach. I leaned down, just enough so he could play with my breasts.

He kept licking and then undid my pants. We maneuvered, and then he was standing again, and I was left in my panties, his lips on my breasts, sucking, the sensations going straight to my pussy.

"I have a condom in my bag," he whispered, the growl tightening my core.

I looked up at him, blushing. "You always carry a condom with you?" I asked. "Not that I'm judging. Because I like safe sex, I like sex period. And I really want to have sex right now. I can't believe I'm talking so quickly or even saying any of this out loud."

"I kind of like you talking out loud like this. I didn't expect it, but I should have. As for the condom, I always keep a few in my bag. Mostly because my roommate in college went on to be an obstetrician, and his mother always used to hand us condoms, making us promise we'd carry them with us at all times. It became a thing."

That made me laugh, and then I groaned when he slid his hands over my panties.

"I'm so fucking happy that I listened."

"The woman's a saint. I should bake her something. I'll send it to her."

"She'd like that. Especially if you tell her why." He slid a finger inside me, and I groaned.

"Really?"

"Oh, yes, bake her a cupcake, send it to her, and tell

her thank you for all the condoms." He slid another finger inside me. "You're so fucking wet, Dakota."

"I swear I'm always wet when you're around. Even when I pretend I'm not."

"You don't need to pretend with me."

"And when this is over?"

"Don't. We're not going to talk about that." And then he kissed me, slid another finger inside me, and I came.

I rolled on his hand, shaking, and when his lips moved to my breasts again, drawing out the orgasm, my entire body shook, and I was so glad that I was on the desk for support.

"Macon, I need you.

"Oh, thank God," he gasped and then stood back, toed off his shoes, and undid his pants. His jeans fell to the floor after he pushed them over his very nicely rounded ass, and I blinked when he took off his boxer briefs.

"Is that a...?"

He ran his hand over his length, his fingers brushing the piercing at the tip. "My condoms are the good kind, not the cheap brand. They'll work with my ring. Is this okay with you?"

I blinked down at the metal and swallowed hard. "I've never...does it hurt?" I asked.

Macon shook his head. "No, it feels fucking good.

And it'll feel good for you, too. I thought about getting a Jacob's Ladder, but I liked the look of this."

His cock was thick, curved ever so slightly, and only looked *more* lickable with the ring at the end.

I swallowed hard. "I like the look of it, too."

"I'll take it out if you ever want to go down on me," he said, and I laughed.

"Trying to protect my teeth?" I asked, my gaze transfixed on his dick. Seriously, I could not stop looking.

"Well, a guy has to dream. However, with the way you're looking at me right now? I'm not going to last very long once I sink into you."

"Will you kiss me?" I asked, suddenly feeling like everything was going too fast and yet not fast enough. I was bare before him, and everything felt like it all began and ended right here.

Macon nodded, and then he kissed me softly, treating me gently as if I were porcelain.

I hadn't meant to do this. Having sex in my office on my desk.

And yet, all I knew was that it felt right. We had been fighting for so long, pushing and pulling at each other, and yet if we had been at home our first time, doing things gently after a date, after I thought about it for too long, it wouldn't have been the same.

Our first time being in the moment and full of passion?

That was what we needed.

This.

Because everything else about us was on schedules, and there were barely any surprises except for the ones that hurt.

When he pulled away and slid the condom over his length, I licked my lips and then reached out, putting my hand on his chest again.

"Are you sure?" I whispered.

He froze, his cock right at my entrance. "I think that's my line."

"Macon. I want you. I'm just terrified of what's going to happen afterward."

His whole body shook, but he leaned down and captured my lips softly. "I'm never going to hurt you. You and me? We'll figure out what comes later. However, I can walk away right now if you need me to."

"Please don't. Just...just know that I want this, but we also need to go slow."

"Slow, I can do." And then he was inside me, filling me. And I ached. I wrapped my legs around him, met his gaze. We both rocked, our bodies sweat-slick, and it felt like a moment.

I could feel him inside me, his piercing touching me at the exact place I needed him to. I wasn't going to last long, just as he said he wouldn't. But right then, it wasn't about the heat or the caresses or the spontaneity. It was about him and me.

And this moment.

When we moved, and both of us came, my eyes were on his, my mouth parted. All I could think about was him.

I hadn't expected Macon.

I had actively pushed him away.

And I had been wrong.

Oh, so wrong.

Chapter 14

Macon

SOMEHOW, WE FOUND A ROUTINE. ONE WHERE I'D become part of the household, even though I knew I shouldn't be. I wasn't pushing myself away precisely. Far from it. But I knew that I was a guest in Dakota and Joshua's home. And yet, we were finding our normal.

It had been a week, and there had been two more notes. Two messages that nobody could trace to Adam, though we were all sure they were from him. It was only the fact that we didn't know where he lived that my brothers and I hadn't found him and taken care of things ourselves. Because we were following the law, even though it wasn't helping us. I hated that the thought even ran through my mind, but the system didn't always work the way it should.

And Dakota knew that more than most. I hated the idea that she was scared and could be hurt by this man. And that there was nothing I could do for her.

"Mama Cat is washing the babies."

I looked down at Joshua, who was bouncing in front of me. I smiled. I pulled myself out of my thoughts, knowing that I didn't need to think about the future beyond taking care of those in front of me just yet.

I was moving on, finding my place. I wasn't fighting anymore. I wasn't hiding. I was living. I would do anything to make sure that Joshua and Dakota were safe.

"Really?" I asked, kneeling in front of him.

I hated how big I was compared to Joshua, that I hovered. I towered over the kid, so I was constantly kneeling down by him.

"Well, she's bathing Wendy and Darling. Hook and Tink are fighting over in the corner."

That made me smile. We had finally decided that calling them babies one, two, three, and four wasn't working out. So, after watching *Peter Pan*, we had decided to name the babies after the characters.

However, Dakota had said no to naming them Peter or Pan because she'd always had a problem with that kidnapping boy who wouldn't grow up. I figured it had to do more with Adam than anything, but I had agreed. The new Hooks these days were usually all dashing in leather with eyeliner and a suave, debonair attitude, so I figured that's why she went with Hook. Plus, Tink was a pretty good name for the little runt of the crew.

I had a feeling that once we found Adam and figured out the next phase of our plan, I was going to end up with five cats at my home, something I hadn't been planning on. But I didn't mind.

I was an animal person, after all, and who better to have a clowder than a vet?

"I need to go check on them and make sure they're doing okay. Want to join me?"

"Uh-huh," Joshua answered.

"And then I bet you we need to look at your homework before bed."

"We still have dinner," Joshua complained.

"Sure, but you're going to want to play with the kittens all night before your bath time, and I assume that means your homework needs to be done."

"I thought you were supposed to be the fun one," Joshua said, rolling his eyes.

"I *am* the fun one," I argued, taken aback.

"No, I think Nate's the fun one."

I held back a groan. "Do I want to know what he's doing with you when I'm not here?" I asked, a little leery.

"He's teaching me how to make fart noises with my arm."

"Who do you think taught him that?" I asked, shaking my head as I stood up.

"I don't know if I want to know the answers to these questions," Dakota said, her hands on her hips. "We've been home for like five minutes, and already, we're discussing farts?" She laughed.

I looked at her then and felt like I was home. I was sleeping in the guestroom. Although both of us had wanted to sneak into each other's rooms, we had been careful not to. Because if we did, that meant we would be touching each other, making far too many noises when Joshua was only a couple of rooms down.

Though after a week, we might be ready for that. I had plans, and if that meant keeping us very, very quiet tonight, we might just do it.

Her eyes darkened as she looked at me. I had a feeling she knew where my mind had gone.

"Go check out the babies, and then come do your homework. I know you still have one more worksheet to go over that Miss Myra didn't get a chance to help you with."

"It was a lot of homework today. Four whole work-sheets," he said, holding up four little fingers.

"Four?" I mock gasped.

"Four."

"Just like the number of kittens in there."

"I know how to count. I'm not a baby." He rolled his eyes, looking so much like his mother before he skipped over to where the kittens were.

They were getting a little rambunctious, crawling over everything, and while my house was a bit more animal-proof, Dakota's wasn't. I'd soon have to take them back to my place, and I didn't know exactly how that would work.

"Thanks for working with him. Tonight is home-made lasagna but defrosted from my freezer, as well as salad. And he needs to make sure that he eats his greens, or he's just going to glutton up on pasta like I want to and not get a single veggie."

I looked over to make sure Joshua wasn't watching and then kissed her softly. "My mom used to hide veggies in the sauce. Carrots and squash and the like. So we didn't notice."

Dakota's eyes widened, and she shushed me. "Don't say that. He'll know."

I laughed and then kissed her again.

"Macon."

"He's seen me kiss you before."

"True, but we need to be circumspect."

We were both being careful. Too careful. We barely kissed, hardly touched, and pointedly didn't discuss where we were in our relationship. Especially considering that I had practically moved in, we'd had sex once, and had only been on two fake dates. Yet suddenly, it felt like we were a family.

There were reasons we weren't discussing our relationship, and fear of the unknown was the main one. Because if we discussed it, then somehow it was real, and then we'd have to deal with the ramifications of that.

"I'll go help him with his worksheet, check on the kittens, and then we'll be ready for dinner."

"Sounds like a plan," she said, and I looked at her face, frowning.

"What is it?"

"This feels so easy, and I don't know how I feel about it."

I nodded, grimacing. "My thoughts are going down that same path, so let's not talk about it right now," I replied quickly.

"Oh, good. We'll just sit in denial and pretend like nothing's happened. Sounds like a great plan."

I kissed her gently on the lips and then narrowed my eyes. "For this exact moment, we can do that. But we're going to talk, Dakota."

"I know. Soon. One day."

And then she scurried off and went to make dinner. I didn't blame her.

I was the one who'd been thinking that I didn't want

to talk because some things would get real. And then I'd just put it on the table like that?

I was seriously losing my mind.

We took the kittens back into their area, and I knew I would have to figure out how to keep them all in one place soon. Mama Cat was already taking over the rest of the house, and the kittens were following. However, Dakota wouldn't be happy if they started using her furniture as scratching posts more than they already were.

"Okay, Joshua. Help me clean up the litter box, and then we'll wash our hands and get to that worksheet."

"Or we could just not do our homework," Joshua said.

"No can do. I already did mine, and I have more after you've gone to bed. If I have to do mine, you have to do yours."

Joshua's eyes widened. "But you're an adult. You have homework?"

"Yes, that's the sad secret that they never tell you. You have homework even when you're an adult and have a job."

"But it's horrible."

"Not all the time. Once you find what you're good at and what you like, sometimes, the homework doesn't feel so bad. It just feels like you're prepping so you can like what you do even more later."

"Maybe. I still don't like it."

"Let's see your worksheet. Maybe I'll agree with you."

We finished with the cats, washed our hands, and then went back to the kitchen table to work on homework.

Dakota hummed as she cooked, working on her own paperwork at the same time as I got up to set the table with Joshua after we finished his worksheets.

We felt like a family as if we did this every day. I should feel scared, as if it had all come on too fast. But the fact that it felt right?

That scared me more than anything.

Joshua ate all of his lasagna and most of his salad, and I did my best not to mention that I knew there were extra veggies in the sauce. I was full by the time we were done, and did dishes while Dakota bathed Joshua and got him ready for bed.

I checked in on the cats, made sure everybody was at least in some semblance of where they were supposed to be in that part of the house, and then went to say goodnight to the little boy that had captured my damn heart.

Dakota read him a story while I stood in the doorway, and it felt right. I'd almost died before, had thought that that would be the end of everything. And I realized I hadn't lived enough. I'd worked so hard on my career, at keeping my little sister safe, that I hadn't enjoyed my own life.

And now I wanted it. I wanted this. I was going to fight for it. Even if that took a lot of convincing when it came to Dakota.

Joshua dropped off quickly, and Dakota and I tiptoed out, turning off the light as we did. The door snicked closed, and I followed Dakota back to her bedroom.

"He's out like a light."

"I'm pretty tired myself," I said.

"Oh. Should I check on the cats?" she asked, her hands fidgeting in front of her.

I shook my head. "I did earlier. They have the run of the back of the house, and I'll check on them in a bit. We closed up the rest of the house, and the detective hasn't called, so we're in for the night."

"I wish we could get an update on Adam."

"There hasn't been a note in two days, and the detective isn't very forthcoming with any helpful information."

"That's been the gist of it. He's never liked me."

I held back a snarl. "He's an asshole."

"I know, and I'm trying to stay calm for Joshua's sake. But inside, I'm screaming, and ranting, and raging."

"I'm right there with you."

She looked at me then and licked her lips. "You are, aren't you? It's so weird, it feels like you've always been here. And it's terrifying."

I moved forward and brushed my knuckles down her cheek. "I was thinking the same thing."

"It's been so hard to sleep with you so close to me yet not close enough." She blushed, the heat of her skin warming my fingers. "I can't believe I said that out loud."

"It's taken everything within me not to creep over here and have my way with you, but I wanted to make sure you were ready. And I didn't know when you would be."

"I think Joshua is passed out, his door's closed, and if you close mine, I'm ready."

"We'll have to be very careful. Very quiet. Any loud sound, and he'll likely wake up."

"You're the one who shouted my name as you came," she teased.

"Excuse me, you did it first."

"I can be quiet if you can."

And then I closed the door, locking it.

"We'll unlock it after. In case he has a bad dream."

I nodded. "After." And then I was on her. I couldn't wait. I wanted this to be slow, soft, sweet. Romantic. But it wasn't going to be. It would be hard and fast and needy. And when she tugged at my shirt, nearly ripping it off my body, I knew she needed this, too. She pulled my shirt over my head, and I did the same with hers.

We practically tripped over one another until we were on the bed, naked, me hovering over her as I played with her breasts, and she wiggled out of her pants.

"I talked to Myra, and we found condoms for you."

I froze, looking down at her. "You talked to Myra about my dick?" I asked, flushing.

"I needed to make sure I had the right condoms in my bedside table. And Myra was here, so it just came up."

I blinked, trying to process. "Oh my God. Do the rest of the girls know I have my dick pierced?"

"I'm not going to lie to you."

I burst out laughing, and she put her hand over my mouth. My eyes widened.

"Don't. He's going to hear you."

"I can't believe you told her," I mumbled against her lips.

"Paris was the one who helped find the condoms," she whispered.

Mortification rolled over me even as my dick twitched at the thought of being so close to Dakota. "Well, that's it, I'm never going to be able to face the girls again."

"If it helps, they were delighted to hear about it. Surprised, but intrigued."

"For the love of God, if you tell me that any of my brothers have their dicks pierced, I am walking right out that door and never looking back."

She put her hands over her mouth as she giggled, and I glared at her.

"Dakota."

"They didn't mention it. And the only person that I know we haven't seen evidence of in the group is Nate. So, he may have a secret piercing for all I know."

"Please stop thinking about Nate's dick."

"You're the one who brought it up."

I pushed my hips against hers, and she moaned. "Speaking of things getting up," I teased.

"That was horrible."

I kissed her, biting at her lip. "You started it," I growled.

"I'm very sorry. I was trying to bring up the fact that I have a condom so you could fuck me."

"I love when you talk all dirty. Miss sweet and sassy."

She licked her lips. "I used to work in a kitchen when I was a teen. I learned all the dirty words."

"Why don't you use them on me?" I mumbled.

And then I was kissing her again, both of us naked, our bodies pressed against each other's. I helped her slide the condom over my dick as I lay on my back, her hovering over me.

"I want this in my mouth," she whispered.

"I've already tasted your pussy. One day, I'll let you taste my cock."

"I'm happy you whispered that," she moaned.

"If you're not careful, I'm going to make you scream."

"You can try," she teased.

And then I took her by the hips and slammed her down on my cock.

I pressed my hand over her mouth to keep her scream muffled, and her eyes widened and then rolled to the back of her head. She clenched around my cock, coming from just the motion, and I groaned, doing my best not to come right along with her.

I lowered my hand, and then she leaned over me, her breasts right in front of my face.

I licked, sucked them each into my mouth as she rode me, both of us breathing in pants as we tried our best not to shout.

When I was close, I pulled out of her and flipped us over so she was on all fours in front of me, and then I slammed home again.

My hands dug into her hips as she pressed her face into the pillow, her moans and words muffled by the fabric.

I bit my lip, doing my best not to make any noise, but it was hard. She was so wet, the sounds we made rough and echoing throughout the room.

We were being as quiet as we could, but not silent enough.

I kept moving, and when she pressed back against me, I swung my hand around and flicked my finger over her clit. She came again.

This time, I followed her. As I did, I leaned over her, moaning into her back, doing my best not to be loud.

I pulled out, leaning against the headboard as we both positioned ourselves so we were lying face-to-face.

"Oh my God," she whispered.

"Yes. That."

I kissed her again, gently running my hands over her body and in between her legs.

"Again?" she whispered.

"Maybe," I mumbled.

And then I moved so my head was between her legs. I licked her up, just needing her taste. It was the only way to keep me quiet, by keeping my mouth on her pussy.

She came again, this time moving a pillow over her face. I grinned, licking and eating my fill.

Afterward, I cleaned us up and unlocked the door before slipping on my jeans. She slid on her pajamas.

"Should I go back to the guest room?" I asked, unsure of what I wanted the answer to be.

"He's already seen you wake up beside me twice. Maybe you should go grab your pajamas and come back."

I looked up then, wondering what I might see, but the mask of Dakota's fear was right back in place.

I nodded, knowing we didn't need answers just yet. We could take this slowly, even as we were careful.

I grabbed my pajamas, slid them on, did my best not to worry about tomorrow, and then slipped back into bed next to her, holding her close.

She fell asleep first, and I listened to the sounds of her breathing before it lulled me to surrender.

I should've remembered that I did not get happily ever afters.

I didn't get peace.

I should've remembered that my nightmares were real.

I had lived them, and they were not letting go.

Chapter 15

Dakota

THE GROAN WOKE ME, PULLING ME FROM MY DREAMS OF heat and Macon. I turned over, only to sit up sharply as I looked over at the man next to me in bed. He tossed and turned, his fists clenched at his sides, his jaw gritted so tightly I was afraid he might crack a molar.

I didn't know whether to wake him or let him sleep through the nightmare. I knew you weren't supposed to wake sleepwalkers, and I always tried to wake Joshua out of his bad dreams—but this seemed like a night terror.

Would trying to help make it worse?

When Macon whimpered and whispered Cross's name, I knew I needed to wake him up. I soothingly put my hand on his shoulder. "Macon. Baby. Wake up. You're safe. I'm here. You're okay."

He didn't wake. Instead, he thrashed again, sweat covering his body and the sheets.

Tension slid through me, and I bit my lip. "Macon."

He sat up, his fist coming at me. I ducked, but I needn't have bothered. He stopped his motion before he got even close to me. His eyes went wide as he stared as if not seeing me until he blinked.

"Jesus Christ. Are you okay? Did I get you?" His voice was gruff as if he had been screaming in his dreams and had somehow ravaged his throat.

I let out a breath and then tentatively put my hand on his cheek. He flinched, and my heart broke just a little. But then he leaned into the touch and let out a breath.

"Dakota. Did I hurt you?"

I shook my head, grateful for the light coming through the curtains so he could see me. "You didn't even touch me, Macon. You weren't close to me. I promise. I was afraid to wake you in case something happened, but when you kept thrashing, I knew I needed to pull you out of your dreams. You're safe. I'm only sorry I startled you." My pulse continued to race, but not out of fear that he'd have hit me coming out of his nightmare, but because there was nothing I could do to make them go away completely.

"Jesus, Dakota. I could've hurt you."

I kept my hands on him, needing to anchor myself as much as he did. "But you didn't. You're the one who was hurting. I'm so sorry. You don't have to talk about it if you don't want to. We both know that sometimes nightmares don't need to be spoken aloud."

Macon stared at me, blinking away his sleep, or perhaps the nightmare he struggled to pull himself away from completely. "I don't know what I was dreaming. Not really. But they're usually the same each time."

I kept my hand on his face and his chest, needing to touch him and know that he was whole. I hoped maybe he needed my touch, as well.

"I'm sorry," I whispered, not knowing what else to say.

Macon shook his head. "No need to be sorry," he said softly. "I know you've been through hell and back."

"Perhaps. But we all have our versions of hell. It doesn't make anyone's less traumatic."

He stared at me for a long moment before he pulled away slightly, his eyes going blank for a bit as if he were pulling up memories instead of staying in the here and now. "I remember everything about that day. I know they say sometimes you forget the most painful parts of your life, that your body and mind protect you. But that's just bullshit." He let out a laugh that held no humor.

"I remember things they told me I shouldn't, either," I whispered.

He met my gaze, the pain in his eyes palpable. "You understand. Not a lot of people would, but you do." He reached out and tucked my hair behind my ear. He leaned forward and kissed me gently, and I pressed into him, knowing that he needed the touch as much as I did.

He pulled away and then let out a breath. "You know, other than Arden being sick, we had a normal life growing up. Nothing too scary."

I looked at him and let him speak, knowing he needed to get it out.

"Arden was sick a lot as a kid, although I don't know if it was just a weak immune system, or if her lupus had flared even then. Most people say you don't deal with things like that until you're older, but I don't know. She was pretty sick when we were growing up. It only got worse after she got older and we tried to figure out how to help."

"She's doing better now, though." At least, I hoped so. I didn't see Arden as much as the rest of Macon's siblings, but when I did, she was always smiling, if a bit tired sometimes. But perhaps she was far better than the rest of us at putting on a brave face during the pain or when the world seemed to be breaking around us.

"She is, with medicine, therapy, and being kinder to herself in the way she lives and endures. She closed herself off from the rest of the world for so long, and it wasn't until she met Liam that she finally found a way out—if only for a little while." He shook his head. "She wouldn't let us pull her out. She hid from us just as much as she hid from the rest of the world, and I hated that I couldn't help my baby sister. That I couldn't help her find her place in the world. That I wasn't able to hurt anybody that dared to come after her."

"You're a good big brother. She knows that."

"Perhaps. But I didn't always feel that way. Cross got angry. Prior tried to be the funny one and make her laugh. Nate is her twin, so they've always had a special connection. And I was the silent one. Even before the shooting. I've always been a little quieter than the rest of them, and I never really knew why. When I was younger, I thought perhaps it was just because I had settled into my skin before the others. And maybe I had. I've always been comfortable. I found my place and my passions and moved on in life. I figured out early on that I couldn't break the world in order to save my sister, so I did my best to be there when she needed me, and not hover as much as Cross did."

"I've seen the way you are with her. You guys are a unit."

"We are. And our parents were always the same. The fact that Dad got that job and moved with Mom was probably the hardest thing they've ever done. They didn't want to leave their baby girl."

"Or the rest of you," I said.

He snorted. "That's true. I've always known that my parents love me. That's never been a problem."

I tried to ignore the hurt at that. Because I knew my parents didn't. Or at least they didn't have the right kind of love. The type that would've let them stay and raise me in a loving and caring home.

Macon frowned. "I'm sorry," he whispered. "I didn't mean to make you think of your parents. Or to make it seem like my family is on some pedestal."

I shook my head quickly. "This isn't about me. And, honestly? I like knowing that there are good families out there, even if mine wasn't the best."

"I'm sorry," he said again.

"Really. Don't be. This isn't about my childhood; it's about you." He didn't say anything for a moment, and I pressed my lips together, not wanting to push him in any direction.

"I had a good life, Dakota. Then everything changed. And I don't know how to get back to the man I was before. Or if that's even possible or something I want." He let out a sigh, ran his hands through his hair and sat up, resting his forearms on his knees. I sat cross-legged next to him and listened, not knowing what else to do that might help.

"Do you want to talk about your nightmare?" I asked, knowing he was circling in other directions because he didn't want to dive too deep. And I was fine with that, but I also wanted him to know that I was here for him.

He looked at me then, the moonlight sliding over his face. Then he reached out and gripped my hand. "I remember every scream. I remember the feel of the air on my face when I walked into that building—the sense of confusion and near foreboding as I walked in with Hazel. I remember the smell of metal, of burnt flesh. I remember the pain—all of it. Hazel's ex shot me because I was in the way. He and Cross's former partner tried to take my life because they wanted Hazel or money or whatever the hell they wanted that they put above my life. And I wasn't even a blip on their radar."

I didn't say anything. Instead, I just leaned into him, letting him know that I was there. I knew the details of what had happened. I'd nearly lost my best friend because of the shooting. And I'd almost lost Macon and Cross before I even truly got to know them.

Macon continued. "They dragged me out to the back of the building. I didn't know what their plans were beyond wanting me out of the entryway. I tried to crawl away after they left, likely deciding I was too heavy to take any farther, but I didn't have the strength. When Cross came, I remember him screaming and saying my name. I have flashes of it all." He paused, and I squeezed his hand, my heart breaking all over again as he recounted the tragic event. "And then Cross left after I told him to go. I knew right then that I was going to die. That no one would be sitting next to me as I faded into whatever existence comes after this one. And I made that choice. To tell Cross that he needed to go and find Hazel. That he needed to save her."

"And I'll always be grateful that you were there to help save my best friend," I said, tears sliding down my face as I placed my palm on his cheek. "But I also hate that you had to make that choice. That I almost lost you before I even got to know you."

I hadn't meant to admit that part, but I knew it was the truth.

I was falling in love with this man. I knew, down to the depths of my soul, that I needed him.

And yet, this wasn't the time for that. I shouldn't and *couldn't* fall. It would be a mistake.

But it wasn't as if I could stop myself.

"When the paramedics came with Cross's neighbor, that's when I started to fade a bit. I was in and out of consciousness, but I remember the parts I was awake for.

The fact that I threw up and tried to apologize even as they put an IV in to send me to sleep."

"I'm so sorry," I whispered.

"I'm sorry, too. That I wasn't able to save Hazel, but I am glad that Cross was there to do it. I hated that there was so much blood. That Cross had to start his business and his life basically from scratch all over again because of someone else's actions and choices."

"But they weren't yours," I said. "It wasn't your fault."

"I know that. I think it took me a while to talk it out with my therapist and realize that what happened wasn't my fault. That I didn't have to be strong enough to protect Hazel. That I did the right thing."

My brows furrowed. "You thought you needed to be strong enough to protect her yourself?" I asked, confused.

"I think some part of me thought I needed to be stronger than a bullet, or faster, in order to stop the man from hurting her. It was the same idea I had where if I had been strong enough, maybe my brother wouldn't have nearly died."

"Macon," I began, but he shook his head.

"I know. It doesn't make any sense. But I don't think it's supposed to. I can't help where my mind goes. And talking it out with my therapist has helped over time. But I still have dreams. So many fucking nightmares."

"But not every night," I said, knowing I had to be right as this wasn't the first time he'd slept next to me. Or perhaps it was only a deep-seated wish that he not suffer each and every night. I hated the idea that he was in pain every day, and hoped that he could rest at some point.

"True. Not every night. Sometimes, it's worse than others, though. This was my first one under this roof. I'm just sorry you had to witness it while sleeping next to me."

"I'm sorry that you have them at all. It doesn't seem fair," I said.

"I'm still here. I suppose that has to count for something."

I reached out and cupped his face. "True, but I wish I could take away your pain. You've done so much for me. For Joshua. I just wish there was something I could do for you."

He leaned forward and took my lips. "Just be with me. That's all I need. Let me know I can stay."

Always.

I didn't say it. I wanted to. But I was so afraid.

Because what would happen when we took care of Adam and we were safe? What would happen when there wasn't a wolf knocking at the door?

But I didn't think that. Instead, I leaned forward and pressed my lips to his.

He kissed me back, a little harder than usual, and I let him. He needed this moment, this touch, and if I were honest with myself, so did I.

Macon lowered me to my back and hovered over me, taking my lips. I let my hands drift up and down his back, soothing him even as I did the same for myself.

He deepened the kiss, angling my head to capture more. And then his lips trailed down my body, and he tugged my tank top away from my breasts, lapping at my nipples, sucking at them. He pinched the turgid points, the sensation going straight to my core. I arched into him, needing him more. He shoved off the tank top completely, my breasts falling free, and he kept playing, pleasuring.

He licked down my belly, biting at the waistband of my pajama pants. When he pulled them off, along with my panties, he dove between my legs, going down on me as if it had been years since he'd tasted me, and not mere hours.

I wrapped my legs around his shoulders, tangling my hand in his hair. He kept sucking, my pussy tightening as he thrust one finger, and then another. He continued to feast, licking me until I came, my whole body shaking. But when he rose to kneel and pull down his pajama pants, I shook my head. He frowned at me.

"Let me," I said, and then I knelt in front of him,

sliding his pajama pants down his body, and watching as his cock sprang free.

I took him in hand, my fingers barely touching around his girth, and licked around the tip of his cock.

"Be careful of your teeth," he warned.

"I'll be gentle." I teased the ring at the tip. He moaned, sliding his hand into my hair, and I gripped his hip before swallowing him. I was careful, going slowly so I didn't hurt myself or him, but I hollowed my cheeks, humming along his length.

He moaned, his hips moving just a bit before he froze and let me take what I needed—which was only to give him what *he* needed.

I worked him carefully, never letting him exit my mouth fully so he couldn't damage my teeth. I had never gone down on someone with a ring before, but I had the internet and friends who'd helped me figure out exactly how to do this.

I loved having this control, watching him fall into near bliss as I gifted it to him. When he jerked, I pulled back and licked my lips, knowing he was close.

"I have to think about baseball right now because I want to get inside you."

"I want you inside me, too."

I twisted around, handed him the condom that we'd set out, and then moved to my hands and knees. He sheathed himself and entered me quickly.

We both moaned, me biting my lip so I didn't scream, him muffling his exclamation as he leaned over me.

His hands dug into my hips, and I pushed back, needing him to go even deeper. I felt so full, nearly ready to burst, but then he moved, and I could barely think. I met him thrust for thrust, knowing I had never felt this close to anyone before in my life.

He slammed into me again, and I let out a shocked gasp, knowing it was too loud. I stifled my voice with the pillow, arching for him. He kept going, filling me.

But then he pulled out and flipped me onto my back. I let out another gasp, but he was inside me again almost instantly, his mouth on mine. He pistoned into me, one hard thrust after another, and I wrapped my legs around him, needing him.

I came on his cock, and he followed me, silencing my moan of pleasure with his mouth.

I had needed this, and I hadn't even realized until he was inside me, holding me like I was a cherished possession.

I loved this man. I didn't know when I had fallen, but I knew I had fallen hard.

As Macon took care of me, kissed me softly, and showed me how much he cared, I just hoped to hell that caring was enough.

I didn't know if he would ever love me. I didn't know

if he was able to, not after everything that had happened.

I only prayed that what he felt would be enough.

And I hoped to hell that when the danger had passed, he wouldn't leave.

And I wouldn't be left alone.

Chapter 16

Dakota

I MOANED, LETTING MY LEGS FALL TO EITHER SIDE OF ME as I fought myself to stay in this dream. Only I knew it wasn't a dream.

But it *was* the best way to wake up.

I arched, pressing myself into Macon's face. He growled low, and I could feel him smiling against me as he ate me out.

"Best fucking breakfast ever," Macon grumbled before he went back to licking my pussy.

I was utterly sated already, having come more than once this morning, and multiple times throughout the night. I hadn't had a good night's sleep; neither had Macon. It had started with the nightmare, and neither of us had truly slept since. It would be a hard day at work for both of us, but it would be worth it. Because we leaned into each other, touched one another, and had the other in our lives. What more did we need?

"Ouch!" I gasped, then put my hand over my mouth as Macon lifted his teeth from my inner thigh. Joshua was going to wake up at any moment.

We had to be quiet. Oh, so quiet.

"You weren't paying attention to me," Macon rasped before returning to licking and sucking. He needed to shave, his day-old beard scraping my inner thighs, and I loved it. It was harsh and rough against my skin, and it was perfect.

I had never really been a fan of oral sex before. Then I met Macon.

Just the thought of his cock in my mouth made my whole body tighten, and Macon hummed again, twisting his finger just right. I came, putting a pillow over my face.

I heard his rough chuckle as he crawled over me and removed the pillow. His lips were on mine in the next heartbeat. I could taste myself, and I blushed all the way to my nipples. He leaned down, spreading his hand over my chest, cupping my breasts lazily.

My alarm went off, and I cursed under my breath.

"Time to face the morning," Macon grumbled, kissing me again after he'd turned the alarm off.

"I am never going to regret what just happened between us. But I am probably going to regret the lack of sleep just a little."

He laughed, letting his hand slide down to cup me intimately. I moaned, my body a little sore. But he didn't do anything but cup me, as if he needed to touch me. Since I had my hands on him as well, I couldn't blame him.

"I guess we should get ready for the day. But you're right, I'm going to need lots of fucking coffee."

I cupped his face and looked at him, hoping he didn't see what I felt blasted all over my expression. I needed to hold onto my love for him for just a little bit longer until I figured out what I was going to do about it.

"Good thing I own a place that sells a lot of it."

"And damn good coffee, too. You have any of those beans that I like here?"

I rolled my eyes. "You have woken up here how many days, and have had my coffee how many times? Of course, I have the beans you like. I've been mixing them in with mine."

"I knew I liked you for a reason." He kissed me again, and I fell that much more in love with him. "And I wasn't thinking. I think I need caffeine to make thoughts work."

"Same."

"Mom!" Joshua said from the other side of the door. I froze, and then we were off in a flash, Macon headed to the bathroom and closed the door while I quickly pulled on my pajamas.

As I let Joshua in, I leaned down to ruffle his hair, my heart racing at almost getting caught by my six-year-old. Crap. "What is it, baby?"

He rubbed his eyes with his little fist, looking like a disgruntled pelican. "You didn't wake me up. I didn't even hear your alarm."

"I'm sorry, baby. Apparently, I'm sleeping in this morning."

"Does that mean no school?" Joshua asked, his eyes wide and bright.

I snorted. "Nope, buddy. That means we have to get busy."

"Macon isn't in his bed. Did he go home? Or is he sleeping with you to keep you company? And happy?"

I froze and wondered what he had heard from his friends, my friends, or even himself last night. I wasn't going to broach that subject, though, even though Macon and I would soon have to talk with Joshua about what all of this meant. That was something that we'd have to discuss with each other first. Because while both of us had decidedly not discussed our paths or our needs and desires other than in bed, and it might have worked for a little while, it wasn't going to work any longer. Especially not with Joshua's knowing and curious glances.

I pushed aside those worries and focused on what I could deal with in the moment. "Okay, let's go get you breakfast, get you ready for the day, brush your teeth, and do all the good things."

"But what about Macon?"

"I am going to help you do that while your mom gets showered," Macon said, walking out in a towel with his hair wet.

I hadn't even heard the shower come on. He must've taken the quickest shower in the history of humankind. And I was kind of sad that he wasn't going to smell like me anymore. However, going to work or being around any of our friends while smelling like sex probably wasn't the best thing in the world.

Joshua looked between us, and I swallowed hard, wondering what questions were going through his head.

"Is today oatmeal day? Or toast and eggs?" Joshua asked, and I blinked a few times, wondering how my son could be so unflappable.

It was one thing to have Macon be part of our lives in subtle ways. It was another to wake up and find Macon in a towel in my room. Of course, Joshua had already seen Macon sleeping next to me twice before, even if both of those times had been innocent.

Regardless, we needed to talk to Joshua.

But first, we had to talk to each other.

Yeah, because that was so easy.

Macon gave me a soft smile as if he knew exactly where my thoughts had gone, then brushed my hair from my face and followed Joshua to his room.

That made me snort and I realized I probably needed coffee. But first, a shower.

I trusted Macon to watch Joshua as I got ready, and it was so weird. I had spent the entirety of Joshua's life being his sole provider. Yes, I had others in my life that I was learning to lean on, and I'd had the Barkers before that, but in reality, it had always been the two of us against the world.

I had thought that perhaps I would feel a sense of loss because it wasn't only the two of us anymore. That, somehow, I wasn't the only person in Joshua's life that he could truly rely on.

But I didn't. Instead, it felt like something had clicked within me, and it just made sense.

I had no idea when that had happened. I added conditioner to my hair, then quickly went about shaving my legs, frowning as I tried to piece together how I had gotten to this point.

I had spent so long pushing people away and showing them that I could do everything on my own.

That I could open a business, be a boss, be a mom,

and do everything all at once. Yet I didn't really feel like that was truly the case.

At least, not anymore. I had failed spectacularly at keeping people out of my life. I was still behind on so much with who I needed to be and who I *wanted* to be, and yet maybe I wasn't.

I owned the business that I worked far too many hours on but loved. And my little boy was healthy, whole, and so smart.

He may hate school right now, but I had a feeling it had more to do with his teacher than the school or the work itself. And maybe we'd find a way to get around that. He already liked working on worksheets a bit more with Myra and Nate and Macon.

I tried not to feel a little disgruntled that he didn't like working as much with me. But I was the sole authority figure in his life. He had to rebel.

I just didn't want him to do it completely.

He was only six years old. Why was I going down this thought spiral?

I rinsed off. I wasn't sure how I felt about the idea that everything seemed to be changing all at once. Perhaps I just needed to let it happen.

I held back a snort. That didn't sound like me at all. I always did things the way I needed them to be done, even if it was the more painful option. The problem was, I loved him. I loved Macon Brady. And I had no idea what to do about it. Because it wasn't just me in this relationship. It would never be.

And, somehow, I had to be okay with that.

No, scratch that.

Somehow, *Macon* had to be okay with that.

I had to figure out where the line would be drawn. How we would be. Only I wasn't sure exactly how to do that.

I never expected Macon Brady.

I never expected how I would feel.

I had gone into this pact for dating because my friends had wanted it so much, and I had simply followed along. Perhaps I had hoped that I could find happiness one day, too. I had thought that maybe I had enough happiness with my son and my job and my life.

Macon was so different, though.

And the girls had set me up with him, even if it had been a façade.

Now what was I supposed to do?

Did I have the patience to follow this path? I wasn't sure. Not with the ever-present terror and fear that was my ex hanging around. That brought me back to the shocking and cold reality of my current situation.

There hadn't been a note yesterday. I didn't know if that meant Adam was done with me or not. Was he lying in wait?

I was so fucking scared.

I let out a breath, then quickly did my hair and got dressed. I could hear the boys getting ready and eating breakfast and talking and having fun. The idea that I had just called them *the boys* in my head, like we were a family, made me pause. I forced myself to stop over-thinking.

I entered the kitchen to get some coffee and nearly fell in rapture as I realized that Macon had already made some.

"Oh, thank God," I whispered.

Macon grinned, handed me a perfectly made cup, and kissed me square on the mouth.

"Do it again! Do it again!"

I turned to Joshua, my eyes wide. "Excuse me?"

"Kiss, kiss!"

"Well, I think we have to do what he says." Macon leaned down, and I pressed my finger to his lips.

"What have you two been up to?" I looked over at Joshua. "Why do you want me to kiss Macon?"

"Because he makes you smile. And I like him. And if he kisses you, then maybe he could stay. And then the cats can stay."

I held back a laugh, and the light in Macon's eyes danced. Of course, it would be about the cats.

I let my hand fall, and Macon kissed me softly, just a chaste peck before going back to the stove where he had eggs cooking and toast in the toaster oven.

"Eggs and toast?" I asked.

"We already ate ours. This is for you. I'm taking the kittens and Mama Cat back to my office today, and then we'll see about some more permanent accommodations."

"You mean here, right?" Joshua asked, a smile on his face.

"Joshua, darling…"

"I know. They can't stay here because we are renting, and it's not our house, and we're never home. But I still want to be able to visit."

"I'm sure we can find a way," Macon said before I could speak up. I gave Macon a look, but he shrugged.

"We haven't found Mama Cat's owners, so it looks like you're looking at them."

I shook my head, my heart breaking and shattering in happiness.

He was just too good for me. And I had no idea why I thought that.

He *wasn't* too good for me. I couldn't let myself believe that I was less than.

And yet, it was all I could do not to lean into him and beg him to stay.

So, I wouldn't. After all, I didn't even know what I wanted for sure.

"Okay, well, it seems that you guys have everything worked out."

"We do. And I'm going to drop this kiddo off at school before I head to work like usual, and you are going to go open up the shop so I can have all the coffee."

"Jason and Pop are opening today. I'm closing."

"Myra's picking him up from school?" Macon asked, and I nodded, taking a bite of toast. It was like we were husband and wife, talking about our son and the day's plans.

I still wasn't sure how this had happened, or really what I felt about it, but I wasn't going to bite my nose off to spite my face. Nor would I run away simply because I was scared. I was done running.

I just needed to make sure that my family was safe. And that meant keeping an eye on Joshua at all times.

I leaned down and kissed Joshua on the top of the head, and then kissed Macon on the cheek.

"I should go."

"Hold on," he said, then made a little sandwich, stuffed it into a baggy, and handed it to me.

"Eat. You're going to need all the caffeine and protein you can get today."

I blushed, thinking about exactly why I was exhausted. I nearly swooned at the memories.

Damn, this man.

I cleared my throat and ignored his knowing gaze. "Are you sure you can handle this morning?"

"I've got this, Dakota. You can trust me."

I looked at him and smiled. "I know I can."

Something crossed his gaze, and I wasn't sure what it was. Was it pride? Or disbelief?

I didn't know, but I knew I had said the right thing.

I said goodbye to my boys, and the cats, and made my way to work.

BY THE TIME I made it through traffic to the Boulder Bean, the place was packed.

"Early morning rush started a bit early," Pop said as she rushed to the back.

I nodded in hello without saying a word, washed my hands, put on my apron, and got to work. I missed opening, but without my babysitters, the others had stepped in, and I had to learn to give in. Jason operated the front, and I worked on orders. We all traded responsibilities often, but I was the fastest at filling orders, Jason was the quickest at taking them, and Pop the best at making sure we had everything we needed. We would likely switch out once the rush was over, with me going back to bake, and Pop and Jason trading places. But for now, this worked.

I barely had time to think of Macon and our relationship, of Joshua's day at school, or the pact with my friends.

The only thing that even hinted at crossing my mind and invading my bubble of bliss was Adam.

But he had always been able to do that. And I hated that he could.

However, I planned to do my best not to let him ruin everything in my life. He had given me the best part of it —Joshua—and I had to remember that.

"Dakota, the school's on the line for you."

I looked over at Pop and frowned, even as a sense of foreboding slid down my body. Chills wracked me, and I swallowed hard, trying to piece together what she was saying.

"The school?"

Pop took the mug and order from me and nodded. "It sounded urgent. Maybe he has a tummy bug?"

I swallowed hard, wiping my hands on my apron as I went to pick up the call on the office phone. I looked in my pocket and realized I had missed three calls on my cell. I nearly threw up.

"Hello? This is Dakota Bristol."

"Mrs. Bristol, I need you to sit down," the woman said, and I nearly passed out. I recognized her voice. Was she the counselor? Or maybe the principal. I wasn't sure, but I couldn't focus. I couldn't think.

"What-what's going on? Is Joshua okay?"

"Mrs. Bristol..."

"It's Ms." I cursed. "That's not important. What's wrong with my son? Where is he?"

A pause. "We're unsure, ma'am."

The floor fell out from under my feet, and a scream echoed in my ears.

My scream.

Chapter 17

Macon

I SAT THERE HOLDING THE WOMAN AS SHE WEPT IN MY arms, her whole body shaking.

"I'm so sorry, Mrs. Roth."

"I'm sorry, too, but he has to be okay."

I nodded, knowing that Coco still had more time. But this wasn't easy. Coco was the sweetest and most precious pug I had ever met. With wide eyes and a sunny disposition. And at even seven years old, it seemed far too young. But he had determination and resilience, and we were going to do everything we could.

The problem was, Mrs. Roth had cancer herself, and

the two of them would be fighting their illnesses side by side. We would do everything we could to keep everybody safe and comfortable and here with us, but I knew it wouldn't be easy. This was the hardest part of my job, and I hated that sometimes I didn't feel strong enough. I just hoped that today we were.

"Excuse me," Jeremy said, clearing his throat.

Jeremy never interrupted during these meetings, nor did I. So I knew whatever he had to say must be an emergency.

"I'm so sorry," Jeremy repeated. "There's a phone call for you, Macon, and you need to take it."

Chills swept over me, and I swallowed hard. "Who is it?"

"It's the bakery. You need to answer the phone. Mrs. Roth? Come on, let me get you some coffee."

"Oh, I hope everything's okay," the older woman said, wiping her tears. "It's Dakota's shop, right? She has the best bakery."

The big small town that is Boulder… Everybody knows everybody else's business, I thought. I made my way to the phone after giving Miss Roth another hug and a tissue and frowned when I heard Pop's voice on the other line.

"What is it?" I asked, my heart racing. Flashbacks hit me, and I pushed them out. This was not about me or my insecurities and memories.

"It's Dakota. You need to get here."

"What's wrong?" I growled.

"She's on the phone with the police right now. The school called. It's Joshua. Someone took him."

My mind went fuzzy, and I tried to catch up. "What?"

"I don't have any answers. I'm just listening to this secondhand. She doesn't even know I'm calling you. I figured she'd call you next, but you just need to be here, okay?"

I was already slipping into my jacket and grabbing my things before she finished speaking. "I'm on my way. Tell her I'm on my way."

"Okay. Just get here. She's so scared."

I didn't tell her that I was scared, too. Though that had to be obvious in my voice. I couldn't process any of it. Because that little boy had to be okay. And if he wasn't? I was going to kill Adam with my bare hands.

I gritted my teeth and looked at Jeremy, who stood in the doorway. "Someone's taken Joshua. Or he left school without telling anyone. We don't know. I need to get to Dakota."

Jeremy's face lost its color. "Go. I've got this. Tell us if you need anything. Do you need me to call your brothers? Hell. Do you need me to drive?"

My hands shook, and I took a deep breath, counted to ten, then remembered what I needed to do to calm myself. "No, I've got this. I'll call in the cavalry on the way. Just take care of Mama Cat and her babies for me, and our patients."

At that, my heart broke again. The kitties needed Joshua, just like I did. Just like Dakota did.

We needed to find him.

"You've got it. Call me if you have an update. Or… fuck, I'll call Cross. Don't even worry about this place. We've got it handled."

I nodded, knowing the practice was in safe hands… and I ran.

MY HEART RACED as I did my best not to drive off the road on my way to the Boulder Bean. I used my Bluetooth to call my family, my hands shaking as I made my way to Dakota.

Cross answered after the first ring. "Hey, Macon. What's up?"

"It's Dakota. And Joshua. I'm on my way to her now. I don't know what happened, but I guess the school said they can't find Joshua."

"What the hell?" Cross sputtered.

"Can you call the family? The girls. I don't know who Dakota's calling; she didn't even call me. Pop did."

"I hope to hell that's not bitterness in your voice."

"You know what? I didn't even have a little bit. Because I know she's not thinking about a phone tree or calling me. She's thinking about her son. Pop got me, and I'll get to her."

"And I'll get the troops. You get to Dakota, see what you can do. And keep me updated if you can. If not? We'll meet you at the shop, or at her home later. Whatever it ends up being. Macon? You've got this?"

"I don't know if I do. If something happens to that little kid, Cross..." I let the words dangle, bile filling my throat.

"He's fine. He's probably just hiding in the playground or something."

"Joshua knows to be on alert. He knows I'm staying at the house because there are dangers out there. He wouldn't just run off."

That had been a tough conversation that I hadn't been a part of, I'd stood at the door, waiting for Joshua to nod his head with wide eyes as his mom filled him in. In the end, we'd tried to make it an adventure for him, an extended sleepover where I would be around. But he always knew not to talk to strangers or go off with random people. He would never hurt his mother like this on purpose.

"Breathe, you've got this. And we've got you. You guys are not alone."

"Thanks, Cross," I whispered, and then my brother hung up, presumably to call the rest of our group.

My hands were slick as I turned the steering wheel

and parked around the block from the Boulder Bean. When I walked in, it was to chaos.

"Ma'am, we're going to need you to go home. We're issuing an Amber Alert. But you need to be home near the phone in case someone calls or he shows up. As soon as we have more information, we'll contact you."

"Dakota?" I asked, pushing through the others.

The authorities looked at me, but I ignored them, my attention on Dakota.

Relief and fear crawled over her face, and she ran to me, wrapping her arms around my neck. She leaned into me for a bare instant, just enough for me to squeeze her tightly before she pulled back, rolled her shoulders, and looked like the woman I had first met. The one with immense strength and a wall between her and the world so no one could touch her. I'd break through that in private and make sure she knew she wasn't alone. For now, she needed that shield so the others didn't see her fear. And I'd let her have it. I needed one of my own at this point.

"Macon," she whispered.

The man in uniform she'd been speaking to came forward. "Sir?"

"This is Macon...he's my...he's mine..." Dakota sputtered. "I mean, he's with me. Macon, someone matching Adam's description was seen around the school. He took him. I know it. He had to have." Tears filled her eyes, and she blinked them away. She was so fucking strong. I hated that she had to be. We'd both break later, but for now, we needed to focus on getting Joshua back.

"Jesus, okay. They're going to find him. We're going to find him." Dakota slid her hand into mine, and I looked up at the other man. "Right?" I growled.

"Yes, we will." The man narrowed his eyes. "I remember you."

"Yeah, I remember you, too. Thanks for your help in saving my life."

Dakota's gaze moved between the two of us, and I shook my head. "He was there that day. Don't worry about it. Now, what do we do?" I asked the familiar man, though I couldn't remember his name.

"Right now, we have the description of the perp and the vic, and we're taking statements from others. Can you tell us where you were?"

Dakota raised her chin. "Macon doesn't have anything to do with this."

I squeezed her hand. "It's fine. It depends on the time, but I've been at my vet practice all day. And I was never alone because we were pretty busy. Surgeries and checkups mostly."

"Okay, I just needed to ask."

I gave the other man a tight nod. "I get it, just find him. He's got to be scared. He's never met Adam."

"He doesn't even know what he looks like," Dakota

said. "I don't even know how he could have found out what Joshua looks like," Dakota repeated.

Adam. Adam didn't even know what his son looked like.

"We're going to find him, ma'am."

"Please stop calling me ma'am. That's not helping," she spat.

I squeezed her hand, and her whole body shook.

"Go home and wait for a phone call. Or a visit. We'll send people with you. There's nothing you can do here. You're welcome to keep your business open, but I figure you might want to sit at home and wait."

"We'll take care of everything here," Pop said.

"I promise," Jason began.

"We've all got it," some of the customers said from around us, and tears filled Dakota's eyes. She blinked them back again.

"You find that baby boy," an older woman chimed in from behind one of the tables. "We'll take care of your shop. We'll make sure everything gets handled. You just take care of yourself and Joshua. We love seeing him when he comes around. And you are such a good woman. You always know what we want and remember all of our names. You care. We care about you. Now, go find your son."

Dakota's small part of town had rallied around her in an instant. Somehow, she'd made connections when she hadn't thought it possible, and I was so fucking proud of her. But for now, I knew this shell-shocked version of the woman I loved needed to be at home and near the phone.

We had to find Joshua.

And the family Dakota had created out of ashes would help her along.

"HOW DID THIS HAPPEN?" Dakota asked as she began pacing in the living room, Tink curled in her hands.

As we left the Boulder Bean to come home and wait for news, word had got out among our little community, and people were coming in, ordering coffees, trying to support her as much as they could. They were also searching for Joshua, as was everybody else. But the authorities had relegated Dakota to sitting at home as they searched and kept an eye on the place, coming in and out often.

So, I was here, too.

Jeremy had dropped off the kittens and Mama Cat, as well as a casserole that Marni had put together. I didn't think anyone would be eating, but Marni had needed to do something with her hands, and I appreciated the gesture.

So now we were at the house, the other three kittens climbing around on my feet as Mama Cat watched us all, the tension in the room almost palpable. At any moment, an officer could come in, ask more questions, and add more pressure to the situation. They were giving us space to breathe while we waited for news, but the break wouldn't last long.

"I want to be out there, looking for him. But Adam is going to call you, I just know it. And that means we need to be where he might show up." It was the line of thinking I'd let myself go down, though I wasn't sure if it was at all rational.

"What if he doesn't?" Dakota asked as she leaned down and rubbed her cheek on top of Tink's head. Tink mewed and stretched at Dakota's touch.

"He's going to. You know he wants money from you or your bakery or something. But he's not going to get any of that."

"I'll give him anything he wants to get Joshua back."

"I know, baby."

"I hate this," she said before she looked through the back windows into the trees beyond the yard. There was a small forest behind her house. The place backed up to the mountains, and there were trees with darkness. It was hard to see beyond it.

I never felt like anybody was watching me from here, but I knew that Dakota sometimes felt that way. Was it because of Adam? Or her past?

I didn't know, but I hated that she looked so lost right now.

That Joshua wasn't here to crack jokes or talk about farts.

I missed that kid so fucking much.

There was nothing I could do but stand here. The others would be by shortly. Soon, the place would be overrun. But maybe Dakota needed the noise. I didn't know what I needed, only that I was so afraid that we weren't going to be able to find him in time. I didn't know what Adam had done to her in the past, and I was afraid that he had only gotten worse with his jail time.

"Does Adam have a family?" I asked.

"I already talked to the police about that." She sounded so off, and I hated it. But I wasn't sure what else to do. I was just as lost as she was.

"Can you talk to me about that?" I asked, my voice soothing.

"Of course," she said, running her hands over her face. "I'm sorry. I kept so much from you, and I didn't even mean to."

"Dakota." I moved the cats back to the box and took Tink from her, putting the kitten with her siblings. I cupped Dakota's face and then kissed her softly. "It seems like the two of us have been together for ages, at least to me."

"You're not alone in that."

"Good," I said, oddly relieved. "While it may seem like that, we're still getting to know one another. We might have been circling each other's lives for a while now, thanks to our friends, but we're still learning the basics. And us being thrown into these weird situations has caused us to skip a few steps. You know my family because you're friends with them. But you haven't met the guys I've been in the ring with yet. You've barely met Jeremy, and you talked to him for the first time really earlier. We're still getting there."

"I know," she said, letting out a breath. "Adam's older than I am. A little too old for back then. I met him when I was sixteen, and he was twenty."

"Jesus." I sighed.

"Your parents are amazing. And you know mine weren't the best. They left me when I was fifteen. Just packed up and left because they were tired of being parents."

"I knew you were young, but...fifteen?"

"Fifteen and a decently young teenager at that. I was good at school, but I was too young to drive or have a job besides working in kitchens under the table and things. It wasn't the best life, but I thought I was doing well. But my parents didn't like that boys started to pay attention to me, and so did their friends."

I clenched my jaw. "Did they...?"

"No, nothing like that. I know some of our friends

have dealt with things like that, but not me. I was lucky. However, guys noticed me. Adam noticed me. He was far too old for me, but I didn't care. It was part of the allure. I fell for him hard. He did drugs, so I tried them."

I nodded, but she shook her head.

"Just weed for me. And just once. It made me sick, and I never did it again. Everyone made fun of me and called me names, but I didn't care. I stayed in school for as long as possible, and I was the driver when everybody was too stoned or drunk to do anything. In the end, between jobs and life, I didn't finish school."

"You didn't have a support system, how were you supposed to?" I asked. "Did you think I was going to judge you for that?"

"You went to veterinary school. You have your practice."

"And you have your own business. Who cares?"

"You surprise me sometimes. Then again, I shouldn't be surprised when it comes to you."

"What happened?" I asked.

"I couldn't work and deal with life at the same time while going to school. I was sleeping on people's couches and staying with friends. The neighborhood we were in, nobody cared that I didn't have a family. The school didn't check in. Child Protective Services didn't even notice. Nobody noticed or cared."

"I could kill your parents."

"They don't matter. I have no idea where they are or if they're even still alive. They don't know Joshua exists, and I'm a better person for it." She paused to let out a breath. "I got pregnant when I was nineteen, had Joshua when I was twenty. During that time, Adam got worse, started dealing hardcore and playing with his version of gangs. They were running other things, too. I think guns, maybe, I don't know for sure. I was working eighty-hour weeks and on my feet, even six months pregnant. The drunker and higher Adam got, the more violent he became until finally, he kicked my stomach."

"Jesus," I muttered. I already wanted to find this man and beat him to a pulp, and her words just made it worse.

"I was fine, I went to the free clinic to get everything checked out, but I was bruised. I had a black eye, and a busted lip. And I realized I was done."

"Did they help?"

"Most of them didn't care. The adults around me just saw this runaway teen from the backwoods without a future. Most didn't offer to help. But one lady did. She helped me get in contact with the authorities. That's how I ended up with the detective that I hate, but he did help. He may treat me like shit, but he did what he could to get Adam behind bars."

"How did he treat you like shit?" I asked, even angrier than before.

"I was a means to an end. Adam didn't get sent away because he hit me but because of the drugs he had on him—hence why the sentence wasn't long enough. They didn't get him for any of the weapons or running either. But they got what they could. And me alerting the police helped them put him behind bars. So, Adam blames me. But I got out of it what I could. I got my GED. I had Joshua, I met the Barkers and was able to scrounge up enough for the Boulder Bean. I thought we were doing well. I thought I could have a future. And now, Adam's back, and my son is gone. And I don't know what I'm going to do."

I leaned forward, touched her face, then kissed her softly.

"You are so strong. You did all of that on your own when you didn't need to. But you're not alone now. We're going to find your son. We're going to find Joshua. We're going to make sure Adam never gets a chance to do this again, and then we're going to think about futures and everything that you and I can do together. Because, Dakota? I'm not letting you do anything else on your own ever again. I'm always going to be here."

I hadn't meant to declare as much as I had, but I needed to. Dakota needed to know that she wasn't alone.

But it hurt to think that I couldn't do more than that. That I couldn't help.

She was hurting, and there wasn't much I could do.

"Macon m—"

"Dakota! Where the fuck are you?"

Dakota turned, looking at the window.

"Adam?"

"I'm going to get the cops in here."

"Don't fucking call the cops or he's dead."

I looked down at my phone, then at Dakota, and the two of us ran towards the back door, afraid of what we might see.

"Hey there, baby. Miss me?"

Chapter 18

Dakota

BILE ROSE UP IN MY THROAT, AND I FELT ON THE EDGE OF
an abyss.

This couldn't be happening.

Adam couldn't be here.

Where.

Was.

My.

Son?

"Where's Joshua?" I shouted as I stood on the back
porch, Macon right beside me. He held his arm out,
blocking me from moving forward.

I almost kicked at him, slapping at him to stop him from pushing me back, but then I saw the gun in Adam's hand, and my entire world turned on its axis as I tried to take a deep breath and wonder what exactly was happening.

"Wherever the fuck we need him to be," he singsonged, and I almost threw up.

He was high as a kite. That much was clear. I could practically see his dilated pupils from here.

And he was pointing a gun at us.

And I didn't know where my son was.

Suddenly, my brain caught on a word he'd said. *We.* So, there were others with him. Others we couldn't see. Were they with Joshua? Or surrounding the house?

I knew the authorities were near and would come at any moment—it was the only reason Macon had even let me out of the house onto the porch to begin with. But I needed them to get here soon.

I needed them to help me save my son.

"Where's my son?" I asked.

"You mean *my* son?" Adam spat.

I hoped to hell the two plainclothes officers at the front of the house could hear this and would come forward soon.

I just didn't know if they would. The forest dampened some of the sounds from my back yard, and they hadn't been in the house. They had given us time to ourselves while everybody was out searching for Joshua.

And yet it seemed to me like could be close.

I was so fucking confused. I just wanted my boy.

"He's fine. He's just learning a few new tricks."

My blood boiled, and I took a step forward, but Adam clicked his tongue.

"You should listen to the brute beside you and not move... You deserve this and so much more."

"I've done nothing to you. Just leave me alone. Leave Joshua and me be."

"You did everything, Dakota!" Adam screamed. "You sent me to jail. Sent some of my men to jail because you were a stupid fucking cunt and couldn't keep your goddamn lips closed. Oh, you could spread your legs for anybody who came near, and yet as soon as you got knocked up, you decided you were too high and mighty for any of us. You didn't like what you saw, so you went to the cops. We don't fucking do that. You know the rules. You broke our laws, and now I'm going to break you."

"You're going to want to shut your mouth."

I froze at Macon's words, and Adam's eyes narrowed to slits.

I knew this had to be traumatic for Macon—fuck, it was just as bad for me. Except for the fact that Macon had already been on this side of a gun before. I refused to let him get hurt again.

I couldn't breathe. I could barely think. I just needed Joshua secure. I needed Macon safe.

"Is this the new dick you're with? Well, it seems like the 'roids are doing their job on those muscles of his. Must have a tiny little dick for you, though. Don't worry, baby. You'll come back to me. And you'll get all the fucking cock you want."

Bile filled my throat, and I nearly threw up.

"Don't look at me like that. You fucking sent me to prison. You deserve what you're going to get and more."

"Adam," I said calmly, as calmly as I could anyway. "You know that there are detectives all around. They might not be able to see you now, but they will. They're going to be in my house at any moment because they're out searching for Joshua. I'm honestly surprised they haven't found you yet."

Adam rolled his eyes.

"We took care of the two out front. We'll get the rest."

Shock slid through me, mixing with revulsion.

He had taken care *of them?*

I looked at the gun in his hands, then at his eyes, and knew. He'd killed the two police officers out front, what else did he plan to do?

"Let me see Joshua," I said.

"No, I don't think I will."

And then Adam shot.

I froze, fear like an icy wave washed over me, and then Macon was on top of me, pushing me out of the way.

"Macon!"

"Are you hurt? Are you hit?"

"I'm fine," I answered, not knowing if it was true. I was too numb to feel anything.

"What about you?"

"He didn't get me. Has fucking shitty aim."

Footsteps sounded around us, and then someone pulled Macon off me. At least six guys were on top of him then, pummeling and kicking, but Macon was faster, stronger.

These men might have thought they could fight, but Macon *was* a fighter.

I scrambled up, trying to help, but I didn't know what I was doing. I had only taken self-defense classes. I wasn't a fighter. I had told Macon before that I had been on the wrong side of a fist one too many times. I didn't want to see it now. But now Macon was using what he had learned to protect me, to help me find my son.

And I couldn't forget that, even if I hated it.

Someone tugged at my hair, and I screamed, but then Adam was there, pushing me off the porch. I fell to the grass, my fingernails digging into the dirt. I scrambled up, but then Adam kicked me in the side. I let out a breath, pain radiating through my ribs as I tried to get up again.

"You stupid bitch. You deserve nothing. That place that you love with the coffee and all the sugar? That should be mine. You were too busy on your back before to give me anything but that sweet pussy. But now you're old and dry. And that little Boulder Bean or whatever the cute-as-fuck name you decided to call it? That should be mine. You need to know what'll happen if you resist. I deserve every single penny that comes from that place because I was the one who supported you. When your mommy and daddy left, I was the one that put food in your mouth. I gave you everything. And you threw it back in my face."

"You gave me nothing!" I spat, wiping blood from my mouth.

I had nothing left to lose.

Yet I had everything to lose.

Adam hit me again and again.

I could hear Macon's struggles as he fought to come to my side; only it wasn't going to work. There were so many against him, and he was by himself.

Soon, though, I knew the police officers had to come back. They would check in with those on patrol and the ones watching the house and realize that something was wrong. My friends would be here. Others would come.

But I didn't think it would be fast enough.

I tried to scramble to my feet, but Adam hit me in the face with the gun, and I nearly blacked out, blood seeping out of my mouth.

Adam pulled me up by my hair and shook me, and I kicked, scratched, leaving a bloody streak down his face. He hit me again and again.

But he didn't shoot me.

No, he wanted me for something.

Panic clawed at me, and I tried to get away.

Macon was coming for me. I knew he would get there.

He kept moving, quicker, the men behind him down on the ground, all out.

Blood coated his face, his side, his hands.

He had done that for me.

And he was coming for us.

And then Adam raised the gun, and I moved.

I thought of Joshua, thought of my friends, and I thought of Macon.

I couldn't let Adam kill him.

So I moved. I tried to get the gun.

Suddenly, there was a fiery pain in my leg as we both fell. I heard a scream, and then there was nothing.

Chapter 19

Macon

THE ECHO OF THE GUNSHOT FILLED MY MIND, BUT THIS time, it wasn't a dream. It wasn't my past.

I could smell the sharp stench of gunpowder, feel the burn in its wake, but I wasn't standing in the shop nor off the back patio, I wasn't watching my life end.

Instead, I heard a sharp gasp, and then both Adam and Dakota were on the ground.

Dakota wasn't moving, and everything broke inside me. A chasm of death and destruction filled me, and I knew I needed to stop it. I knew I needed to move forward and find a way to think, make sure she was okay, but all I saw was that sniveling piece of a man backing away from Dakota, his eyes wide and vacant.

As if he hadn't realized or couldn't comprehend that he had just shot Dakota.

I roared and went at him. Adam looked at me, his stoned eyes widening comically before he reached for the gun. I kicked it out of the way and leapt on him. I punched him over and over. Adam tried to push at me, to pull free, but he was too weak.

And I wasn't thinking clearly.

I punched harder, hitting him again.

Adam put his hands in front of his face and then kicked and punched. I saw a flash of silver to my right and realized that Adam had pulled a knife out of his pocket. I twisted the other man's wrist, and he screamed in a high-pitched wail before the blade fell into the grass.

The grass now turning a rusty red because of the blood.

Dakota's blood. I needed to go to her. I hit Adam again, one time after another. When Adam finally quit moving, I moved off him, my hands covered in red, and knelt beside Dakota.

She lay there, weak, her eyes fluttering open as she grabbed her leg. I stripped off my button-down shirt, leaving me in a tank, and rolled it into a ball, pressing it against Dakota's calf.

She let out a scream and looked up at me, her whole body shaking.

"Joshua. Where is Joshua?"

"We'll find him. We need to take care of you right now."

"I'm fine. I think I am anyway."

"We'll make sure of that."

Sirens wailed, and I knew that someone had likely heard the gunshot and called, or maybe even they had realized that the plainclothes officers weren't answering their phones.

I didn't care how it had happened, but help was coming.

And then there was a terrified scream, a rustle in the trees, and Joshua ran out, a rope dangling from his ankle. He ran towards us, his hands duct-taped in front of him, his eyes wide, and tears streaming down his face.

"Get him. Get him!" Dakota rasped, her whole body convulsing with sobs.

I stood up, leaving Dakota—the hardest thing I'd ever done in my life—and ran towards Joshua. I picked him up, checked him for wounds, and only saw dirt and a few scrapes around his wrists and ankle. I crushed him close as he sobbed against my shoulder, calling out for his mom and me.

I didn't let myself feel, didn't let myself do anything yet. I went back to Dakota and held the bundle of cloth to her leg as I shouted for the authorities to come to the back yard.

The others I had knocked out were still out cold, thankfully, and I knew I'd have to answer for that. But I didn't care.

I just rocked Joshua as I held Dakota and tried to push out the memories.

Because I knew that no matter how many times I relived the shooting, it would pale in comparison to this. I'd nearly lost Joshua and the love of my life, even though I still didn't know if she would be okay.

People talked to me all at once then, and I answered questions, though I didn't know how.

Somehow, I knew we were going to be all right. Because we had to be. If I lost Dakota after all of this, I would never forgive the world. Never forgive fate.

Because I had just found my future, and there would be hell to pay if I had to give that up.

BY THE TIME we made it to the hospital, Joshua and I riding in the back of the second ambulance behind Dakota's, I was exhausted and ready to go home.

I knew that my house wasn't going to be mine for a while, though. My home would be wherever Dakota and Joshua were. No matter what.

Joshua lay on Hazel's lap, finally sleeping. He would

need someone to talk to, to find some way through everything that had happened today, but physically, he was unharmed. Emotionally? That would take some time.

But we'd find a way.

He had fallen asleep in my lap, then had moved from lap to lap as everyone he loved had held him close, making sure he knew that he was okay and cherished. He woke up crying every once in a while, asking for his mom, and we just told him he would see her soon.

Because, Jesus Christ, he had to see her soon if I had anything to say about.

We would have to deal with the authorities, and they would likely want to know exactly how I had been able to fight off so many. But the fact that I knew how to defend those I loved was something people would have to deal with.

I didn't fire a weapon, didn't even use one. Yet, somehow, we had survived.

Dakota would be okay. Thank God. The bullet hadn't hit bone or anything vital, but it had torn through the muscle. It would take some time for her to recover, and she would hate that because she couldn't be on her feet. We would find a way to make the Bolder Bean work without her, though, or with her in a new position seated behind the counter.

I didn't care about any of that. Not really. All that mattered was that she was okay. She was safe.

And Adam would be behind bars for a long fucking time.

It didn't matter that he hadn't pulled the trigger on those two officers, he had ordered the hit. He would be put away for those murders, for attempted murder, kidnapping, illegal firearms, parole violations, and so much more.

We would never have to deal with him again.

Now, I just needed to make sure that Dakota remained okay.

I hadn't been able to talk to her, mostly because she was still dealing with all of the doctors, and the girls had wanted to go back to see her. Joshua hadn't wanted to leave my side, and Dakota wasn't ready to see her son yet anyway. They wanted to make sure she was all cleaned up, her leg hidden until he knew she would be fine.

I understood that, so if he came back to me, I would let the barnacle hold onto me as I listened to him sleep.

He woke up again, scrambling off Hazel's lap and into mine, and I held him tightly.

"What about the kittens?" he asked, his voice sleepy yet still full of fear.

"We were just there to check on them," Myra said as Nate stood in front of me and ran his hand over Joshua's head.

"Miss Myra and I took care of them. They miss you, but they'll see you soon. You don't need to worry about them. They're part of our family now, so they'll always be taken care of."

A lump rose in my throat at that, and I smiled at my baby brother. He understood what needed to be said. I just wished I was strong enough to find the right words to say to Joshua myself.

"Don't go away," Joshua said, looking up at me.

I shook my head. "I'm never going away, Joshua. I can promise you that."

"Not just never. You have to stay forever."

The others turned away slightly to give us as much privacy as possible, and I leaned down to look at the little kid in my arms. "If I have anything to say about it, I'm not going away ever. I love you, Joshua. As if you were my own son."

There was a sniffle beside me, the sound of someone hushing another, and I ignored them all.

"I love you, too, Macon. I know that man said he was my daddy, but he's not. I want you to be."

My heart nearly broke as another sniffle came from the other side of me. Once again, I ignored them.

"I need to tell your mama a few things first. But, Joshua? I'd love to be your family."

"I'll help you make it happen. You, me, and the

cats." He paused. "But I want you to be family, and not just because of the cats. Because I love you, too."

That did it. Tears fell down my cheeks, and I held Joshua close, rocking him back to sleep as the others around us wiped their faces.

Even Cross wiped his face, his big beard shaking as he let out a sigh.

"That kid is breaking our hearts," Prior said, rubbing his chest.

"Tell me about it," I whispered.

I hadn't meant to fall for a family, but here I was, waiting to see the woman that I loved, and holding the kid that I thought of as my own.

I just hoped that Dakota hadn't been scared off by everything that'd happened. Because I knew how she was. Dakota would build up a wall and try to push everyone away.

But I'd do my damnedest to make sure she didn't do that to me.

Because I loved Dakota Bristol.

And I would do everything I could to make sure she understood that I wasn't going anywhere.

Chapter 20

Dakota

I LEANED BACK AGAINST THE PILLOW AND MOANED. I WAS finally alone. The detectives, the nurses, and the rest of the staff had finally left to give me some time to sleep. Only I couldn't. I wanted to see Joshua. Macon. I wanted to see the family I'd made.

And it scared me to even think that. But I wanted Macon near me.

I couldn't believe I'd been shot. A bullet had pierced my flesh, had torn through my calf muscle, but at least it hadn't damaged anything too vital. I would be left with a scar, and with physical therapy, hopefully, I'd be able to walk as if nothing had happened. But it would take time.

And I would use all of that time and more.

Because that meant I was here. I wasn't gone. I hadn't left my son. I hadn't left Macon.

There was a tap at the door, and I looked up, my heart racing just a bit.

"Can we come in?" Macon asked, that deep voice going straight through me.

I nodded, tears pricking my eyes at just the sound of his voice. "Please," I said, realizing afterward that he couldn't see me nod.

He opened the door fully, and I knew who else was here.

Macon stood there, Joshua in his arms, my little boy leaning on him as if he had been doing it his entire life rather than just the short time we had known Macon.

It had been over a year of having the man in our lives, far longer than my brain even let me admit sometimes. Because Macon had healed since his gunshot wound and was perfectly fine fighting and acting as if nothing was wrong.

I knew he still had nightmares, like I probably would for the rest of my life.

But we were safe—all of us.

And Adam would never hurt us again.

"Baby," I whispered.

"Mommy," Joshua said, his voice small, sounding so much younger than usual.

I held out a hand and then patted the place next to me. I had already scooted over in anticipation of him coming into the room.

The doctors had told me that he was allowed to come in for a short while, but then he would have to go. I needed to sleep and heal. And they didn't want to traumatize him. I was all for making sure my baby was as safe as possible.

Macon came forward and gently placed Joshua on the bed. Joshua didn't touch me. Instead, he just looked down at the blankets and then up.

"Hey, baby. I'm happy you're okay." My voice broke, but I did my best not to cry. He had already seen me broken. I didn't want to scare him today. He had seen me cry before. But I never wanted him to think that crying or weakness was bad. However, after so much in one day, I didn't want to overwhelm him either.

"Are you really here, Mommy?" Joshua asked.

This time, the tears did fall, and there was no holding them back or hiding them. Macon pushed my hair back from my face, and I looked up at him over Joshua's head.

"Thank you," I whispered.

"Joshua, I think your mommy needs a hug. Gently, though."

"I really do," I said, looking down at my son.

He reached up and mimicked Macon's move by brushing my hair back from my face and then wiped my tears with his little hand. I cried harder, and then he gently hugged me as if I were porcelain and then patted my shoulder.

"I love you, Mommy."

"I love you, too, baby boy."

"I'll always be your baby."

That got me. I cried harder and held him close while Macon ran his hands over my hair, and Joshua's. After a few more minutes of tumultuous peace, I pulled back.

"You're okay? I know the doctors told me you were fine. But talk to me, baby."

"I'm okay. I was scared. But everybody's been really nice, and they're not going to let me be alone. I was really, really scared," Joshua said, his little lip trembling.

He had pulled himself from the rope and had run towards his home. I had walked those trails with him in the forest before, and he had found his way back. He had saved himself in the end—my little boy, who was far too strong for his age. Had seen far too much.

And he would be very lucky if I ever let him out of my sight again once we got home.

Macon must've noticed my determination and gave me a tight nod. "Okay, now, Ms. Hazel and Cross are going to take you back to their place. They have the kittens there, too. And Momma Cat," he added.

"I'm going to stay there?" Joshua asked.

"For now. Just for a bit. They'll be with you all night. So will everybody else. It's probably going to be very crowded, and there will likely be a lot of food. And cupcakes."

"I like cupcakes," Joshua said solemnly. He looked up at my face. "What about you, Mommy?"

"I need to stay here for the night, just so the doctors can keep an eye on me and make sure I'm okay."

"I saw a lot of blood. I don't like blood."

I swallowed hard, my hand convulsing at my side. Thankfully, he couldn't see. "I don't like blood, either. But I'm going to be just fine. I might have to walk on crutches or use a cane for a little while, but that won't be scary."

"Mr. Peanut uses a cane."

That made me snort. "He does. I didn't realize you knew Mr. Peanut."

"That's what Macon and Nate were talking about. I don't know. I just remember that I like peanuts."

I held back a laugh, wondering how I could even laugh at a time like this. "Well, that's good, baby. I love you."

"I love you, too, Mommy." He kissed my cheek before giving Macon a careful look and then looking back at me. "And I love Macon, too. We already talked about being a family, so if you can make that happen, that would be great." He scrambled off the bed as I blinked down at him. I saw Cross at the door, his eyes wide. He leaned down and picked Joshua up, giving Macon a nod.

"On that note, I'm going to leave the two of you alone."

"Good night, Mommy. Good night, Macon."

Cross closed the door at Joshua's words, and I looked over at Macon, shaking my head.

"What was that about?"

Macon smiled, sticking his hands into his pockets. "Kid always has to steal my thunder."

"What are you talking about?" I asked, my heart racing.

"You better calm down, Dakota. If you don't, the nurses are going to come in and think you're in trouble."

I didn't care what the nurses thought. I only wanted to know more about the man standing in front of me. The one who had saved my life. "Macon."

He sat down in the chair next to me and took my hand, tracing my palm with his finger. I wanted to reach out and run my hands over his face, over his day-old beard, and just hold him.

"First. If you ever jump in front of a fucking bullet

for me again, I'm going to spank that ass of yours so hard, you won't sit for a week."

"First," I said, my cheeks heating, "we already discussed this kink. We don't need the nurses in here. Second, I'll do whatever I have to in order to protect you, just as you would with me."

"I don't agree," he growled.

"Deal with it."

He looked at me then, his eyes full of something I couldn't decipher before he nodded tightly. "Second, Joshua and I came to an understanding."

Humor and happiness filled me, along with a little trepidation. "Oh?" I asked, cautious.

"He wants us to be a family. And I told him I would do everything I could to make that happen." He looked up at me and squeezed my hand. "And he promised it wasn't because he wants the cats in his life." He paused. "Okay, he promised that wasn't the only reason."

I laughed, actually laughed aloud. I hadn't thought it was possible to do that today, if ever again.

But he made me laugh.

"Are you serious?"

"I am. He wants me to be part of your family. And I'm just fine with that. Because I love you, Dakota. I didn't realize I could feel like this. Ever. You're it for me. You are the family I want. You and Joshua. And I'm going to do everything that I can to let you know that you're it for me. I know it might be too soon, but with everything that happened? I don't know if it's soon enough. I want you and Joshua in my life forever. I don't want you out of my sight ever again. I know that going back to your house might be too much right now, so you can come to mine. Both of you. And the cats. I'll make it work. Or I'll stick with you. I don't know exactly what works or is best for us, but I know I want you in my life. Because I love you, and I never want to spend another night without you."

The tears fell again, and I swallowed hard, looking at him. "I was going to try to find a way to make sure that you knew that I didn't want you to leave. I hoped that this wouldn't scare you away."

He just shook his head. "What the hell could ever scare me away from you? I fucking love you, Dakota. You're my family."

"I love you, too. Of course, I love you."

"You just have to promise to never stand in front of a fucking gun for me again," Macon growled out once more.

"I honestly can't make that promise," I said, my hands shaking. "But let's promise each other we won't get into that kind of situation again. How about that? Because you saved my life. You saved my baby's life. If you hadn't used what you learned in the ring to protect us, Adam may have taken everything."

He shook his head. "That doesn't excuse the fact that I was fighting in some fights I shouldn't have been."

"Maybe not, but I'm not going to ever speak poorly about it again because it brought you to me, and it kept you in my life. And us in yours. So, yes, to whatever you're saying. Yes. I want to be your family. You, me, and Joshua. And the cats. We're a package deal."

"That's what I want, too."

And then he leaned down and took my lips. The nurses came in soon after, the sounds of the alarms on my heart rate monitor echoing throughout the room.

I hadn't meant to fall for Macon Brady, but when I allowed myself to feel again, allowed myself to believe, he'd been right there, ready to catch me as I fell.

I'd promised myself that I'd face the world alone, I'd be the best mother I could be without letting myself become the shambled soul I once was. But I'd been wrong.

Macon had found me, had fought with me, had fought *for* me.

And now, I would spend my days fighting for him, fighting for us…and fighting for our future.

He was my destiny.

And I thanked God I'd finally seen the truth.

Chapter 21

Macon

"THIS IS SERIOUSLY THE BEST SMOKER," PRIOR BEGAN again, and I groaned, shaking my head at my brother's antics. Every time we came to Liam's cabin, Prior went on and on about the smoker. Well, if I were honest with myself, all of us did. Liam had a great setup up here, and I was a little jealous. However, Liam was generous with the keys, and any of his family and most of the Montgomery cousins for that matter, were always welcome. And since Liam was married to Arden, I got to come up and visit, too.

Today was Arden's birthday, and we were celebrating

in style. Many of Liam's family members were here. I couldn't keep all of their names straight, even though I had tried, and there was a flowchart.

There were just too many of them.

However, the entire Brady family was here, even my parents. I had a feeling they might be moving back any day now, considering how our family kept growing. They already had a new grandson in Joshua.

The boys were out in the back now, my father playing catch with Joshua as he giggled and ran around the bases. The *bases* were old pillows that we had found and Liam wasn't too ecstatic about us using, but it worked.

Dakota was talking with Hazel and Paris in hushed tones, and I had a feeling it had to do with a certain pact sister who was not here.

Myra hadn't been pulled into the pact yet, but any day now, she would be forced on her blind date.

She was the last of them, and for that, I was kind of nostalgic.

Their blind date pact had brought the women into our lives, most especially, Dakota into mine.

"You have that cheesy grin on your face again," Cross whispered.

I did my best to wipe it off, but I couldn't.

"I can't help it. I'm happy."

"Now that is the best thing you have ever said." Prior leaned against the railing.

"Seriously, man, that makes me happy, too," Liam added, turning the steaks on the grill.

"I still hate that she's standing on her crutches and not sitting down like she should be," I called over my shoulder.

"It's been two minutes. I'm allowed to stand," Dakota singsonged and then went back to whispering with the other women.

I snorted, and the men just rolled their eyes.

"Women," they all said at the same time and then ducked as random chips started flying.

"We heard that," a few women called from the other side of the porch.

"Was that my woman, or no?" Liam asked.

"No, I think that was either your sibling or cousin. I have no idea how many there are of you," I said, shaking my head.

"It's okay. Sometimes we even wear nametags at family reunions. It's the only reason I can ever figure out who my brother is," Liam added deadpan.

I snorted and took a sip of my beer. "And I thought it was bad with the five of us."

"What are you saying, bud?" Arden said, pinching my side. I wrapped my arm around her shoulders and kissed the top of my baby sister's head.

"That you are the best. Everyone else sucks."

"You know we're standing right here," Prior huffed.

"I like this side of you," Arden chimed in. "My big brother, all nice and happy. Dakota and Joshua are sure making you all smiley."

"It's rather disturbing," Prior replied, shaking his head.

"Hey, don't harp on Macon's happiness." Paris came up on my other side to wrap her arms around Prior. Arden moved to do the same with Liam, and then Hazel was there, hugging Cross. I moved back and gently picked up Dakota so she was sitting on the stool in front of me.

She let me do that, and Prior took the crutches. I was grateful that there were other people around. Usually, she bit my head off.

Dakota did not like being on crutches or asking for help. That much I had known even before they handed her the damn things.

But Pop and Jason were filling her shoes nicely. Dakota was on a fancy little rolling stool in the front now while taking orders, or in the back, dealing with things she could do from a seated position. We did not let her walk around the place on her crutches, and she just had to deal with that.

Later, she'd be in a different position. But for now,

everybody was a little overprotective, and for that, I was happy.

"When do you get the final move-in?" Liam asked.

"Next week. We're putting the house on the market and everything," Dakota said, and I heard the wistfulness in her tone.

"I told you we could change that," I added quickly.

She glared up at me. "You have the bigger house, and it fits the five cats that we now have," she said dryly.

"And the puppy that you're probably going to get soon." Cross sipped his beer. I narrowed my eyes at him.

Dakota growled. "Oh, we'll be getting a puppy. Never."

"You know I'm a vet. Sometimes, puppies just show up," I said.

"You are as bad as our kid," Dakota replied, and I grinned at that.

We were getting good at calling Joshua ours. The second that I had seen Joshua outside of the hospital, he'd called me Dad. I had nearly gone to my knees and wept in front of him, but I did my best to act stoic and fucking ecstatic.

Joshua hadn't wasted any time making sure we were a family.

I was going to get a ring on Dakota's finger soon, and we'd finalize adoption because Joshua was mine, and Dakota wanted no part of Adam anywhere near him. I was just fine with that. But for now, Joshua was ours, and I was theirs.

"Anyway, we're not staying in my house. You know why."

I ran my hand down her hair and kissed her temple. "I'm sorry."

"I know," she whispered.

"You said you were sorry pretty quick." Prior grinned. "It's like a whole new side of you." He let out an oomph as Paris elbowed him in the gut, and then he rubbed his stomach. "Those elbows are pointy."

"I will end you, Prior Brady. This is a nice happy family moment. Don't mess it up."

"Ah, you guys are so sweet," Hazel said with a laugh.

Dakota laughed before she continued. "Anyway, we're moving in next week. And, thankfully, we're still in the same school district, although I'm glad we're not going to be at that school next year anyway when Joshua ages out."

None of us needed to say why. That was where he'd been abducted. Joshua was doing just fine, but he was still a little scared. We were going to therapy as a family, plus all of us individually. And mother and son were going together as a duo, too. Somehow, we were making it work. I had never been one to talk about my feelings, but I learned that I needed to when I was first hurt. Now, I was doing it even more.

"Well, this just makes me happy," Paris said, grinning. "You guys are too cute. And the fact that your parents are in love with that kid there? I'm pretty sure they're going to start asking for grandbabies soon."

"They never ask for grandbabies." Arden shook her head. "They're always very polite about it, but I think they're ready," she said.

"Well, they're welcome to be the most amazing grandparents to Joshua there is. I, for one, am thrilled that they've connected so well," Dakota guaranteed, and I kissed the top of her head.

"Look at us, growing up and having families," I said. "Who would have thought?"

Cross narrowed his eyes and looked around. "You know, there is one set of people who are not in this circle right now. And they haven't settled down."

"I was hoping nobody would notice that." Dakota winced. "Does anyone know where they are?" she asked, and I pulled her closer, hugging the love of my life as I kissed the top of her head once more.

"I have no idea, but soon, we're probably going to hear the shouting. That's how it always starts." I shook my head, putting Nate and Myra out of my mind because I knew they'd figure their problems out. Our group was too solid for them not to.

And, honestly, the only person I needed to focus on

today was Dakota. Joshua was taken care of, and I had the woman I loved in my arms.

Nothing else mattered.

And after a lifetime of focusing on others and months not knowing if I'd make it out of the darkness, the little bit of hope that filled me at the thought of a future with Dakota and Joshua made it seem like the rest had been worth it.

I'd found my happiness.

Finally.

Epilogue

Nate

I looked around the patio, at the groups of people that I should probably be able to put names to, and yet couldn't focus well enough at the moment to figure it out.

My head hurt, and I didn't know if it was from stress or another migraine coming on, thanks to the concussion protocol that never went the fuck away.

I grumbled, knowing I wasn't my usual happy self, but people would have to deal. There were enough people around here with a sense of humor and sarcasm to get the mood going. I would only make it worse.

I got a beer from the ice chest and went back into the house, finding a quiet spot to rest my head, and myself. I was tired. I didn't know how I'd ended up here. I had thought I'd pushed it all away. That I'd been able to be the happy, carefree guy that could handle anything.

And yet, one hit after another, I was back here, wondering why the fuck I was always the one left behind. Why the fuck everything hurt.

I sat in a leather armchair in front of the fireplace and looked at the books in front of me. I could barely even focus on them.

The headaches weren't that bad. Not usually. It just meant that I couldn't drive some days, and I'd had to change my career.

It wasn't the only part of me that mattered.

But I hated that it had mixed with the past. Memories I would rather forget.

As if on cue, the sound of stiletto heels on wood echoed in the hallway, and *she* stood in the doorway, the perfect silhouette of curves and sin.

Of ice and cold.

"We need to talk."

I looked up at Myra and raised a sardonic brow. "Do we?"

"You know we do and why, Nathan."

"I honestly don't," I lied. It felt like it had taken years to get to this point. Decades, even. I pulled my gaze away from her, despite the pain that had nothing to do with my headache. It was always so hard to tear my gaze from her.

I hated her.

With the strength of a thousand fiery suns, I hated her.

Though I think I hated myself more.

"Yes, we do, *husband*."

I flinched, looking over her shoulder to see if anyone was around to hear. "Don't fucking call me that."

Myra just raised her chin, looking like the ice princess she was. "Fine. *Ex-husband*. Whatever title you want to use. But we're going to talk."

Next up in the PROMISE ME SERIES?
Nate and Myra in FROM OUR FIRST
For more information, go to www.CarrieAnnRyan.com

WANT TO READ A SPECIAL BONUS EPILOGUE FEATURING MACON & DAKOTA? CLICK HERE!

A Note from Carrie Ann Ryan

Thank you so much for reading **FAR FROM DESTINED.**

I loved writing this story! I think I fell in love with the chowder and Joshua just as much as I did Macon and Dakota!

Next up? Let's just say things are about to get even messier for Nate and Myra in From Our First.

And in case you missed it, Arden and Liam might be familiar if you read Wrapped in Ink!

And if you're new to my books, you can start anywhere within the my interconnected series and catch up! Each book is a stand alone, so jump around!

Don't miss out on the Montgomery Ink World!

- Montgomery Ink (The Denver Montgomerys)
- Montgomery Ink: Colorado Springs (The Colorado Springs Montgomery Cousins)
- Montgomery Ink: Boulder (The Boulder Montgomery Cousins)
- Montgomery Ink: Fort Collins (The Fort Collins Montgomery Cousins.)
- Gallagher Brothers (Jake's Brothers from Ink Enduring)
- Whiskey and Lies (Tabby's Brothers from Ink Exposed)
- Fractured Connections (Mace's sisters from Fallen Ink)
- Less Than (Dimitri's siblings from Restless Ink)
- Promise Me (Arden's siblings from Wrapped in Ink)
- On My Own (Dillon from the Fractured Connections series.)

If you want to make sure you know what's coming next from me, you can sign up for my newsletter at www.CarrieAnnRyan.com; follow me on twitter at @CarrieAnnRyan, or like my Facebook page. I also have a Facebook Fan Club where we have trivia, chats, and other goodies. You guys are the reason I get to do what I do and I thank you.

Make sure you're signed up for my MAILING LIST so you can know when the next releases are available as well as find giveaways and FREE READS.

Happy Reading!

The Promise Me Series:
Book 1: Forever Only Once
Book 2: From That Moment
Book 3: Far From Destined
Book 4: From Our First

WANT TO READ A SPECIAL **BONUS EPILOGUE** FEATURING MACON & DAKOTA**? CLICK HERE!**

Want to keep up to date with the next Carrie Ann Ryan Release? Receive Text Alerts easily!
Text CARRIE to 210-741-8720

About the Author

Carrie Ann Ryan is the New York Times and USA Today bestselling author of contemporary, paranormal, and young adult romance. Her works include the Montgomery Ink, Redwood Pack, Fractured Connections, and Elements of Five series, which have sold over 3.0 million books worldwide. She started writing while in graduate school for her advanced degree in chemistry and hasn't stopped since. Carrie Ann has written over seventy-five novels and novellas with more in the works. When she's not losing herself in her emotional and action-packed worlds, she's reading as much as she can while wrangling her clowder of cats who have more followers than she does.

www.CarrieAnnRyan.com

Also from Carrie Ann Ryan

The Montgomery Ink: Fort Collins Series:

The Promise Me Series:

The On My Own Series:

The Tattered Royals Series:

Book 1: Royal Line

The Ravenwood Coven Series:

Book 1: Dawn Unearthed

Montgomery Ink:

Book 0.5: Ink Inspired

Book 0.6: Ink Reunited

Book 1: Delicate Ink

Book 1.5: Forever Ink

Book 2: Tempting Boundaries

Book 3: Harder than Words

Book 4: Written in Ink

Book 4.5: Hidden Ink

Book 5: Ink Enduring

Book 6: Ink Exposed

Book 6.5: Adoring Ink

Book 6.6: Love, Honor, & Ink

Book 7: Inked Expressions

Book 7.3: Dropout

Book 7.5: Executive Ink

Book 8: Inked Memories

Book 8.5: Inked Nights

Book 8.7: Second Chance Ink

Montgomery Ink: Colorado Springs

Book 1: Fallen Ink
Book 2: Restless Ink
Book 2.5: Ashes to Ink
Book 3: Jagged Ink
Book 3.5: Ink by Numbers

The Montgomery Ink: Boulder Series:
Book 1: Wrapped in Ink
Book 2: Sated in Ink
Book 3: Embraced in Ink
Book 4: Seduced in Ink
Book 4.5: Captured in Ink

The Gallagher Brothers Series:
Book 1: Love Restored
Book 2: Passion Restored
Book 3: Hope Restored

The Whiskey and Lies Series:
Book 1: Whiskey Secrets
Book 2: Whiskey Reveals
Book 3: Whiskey Undone

The Fractured Connections Series:
Book 1: Breaking Without You
Book 2: Shouldn't Have You
Book 3: Falling With You

Book 4: Taken With You

The Less Than Series:
Book 1: Breathless With Her
Book 2: Reckless With You
Book 3: Shameless With Him

Redwood Pack Series:
Book 1: An Alpha's Path
Book 2: A Taste for a Mate
Book 3: Trinity Bound
Book 3.5: A Night Away
Book 4: Enforcer's Redemption
Book 4.5: Blurred Expectations
Book 4.7: Forgiveness
Book 5: Shattered Emotions
Book 6: Hidden Destiny
Book 6.5: A Beta's Haven
Book 7: Fighting Fate
Book 7.5: Loving the Omega
Book 7.7: The Hunted Heart
Book 8: Wicked Wolf

The Talon Pack:
Book 1: Tattered Loyalties
Book 2: An Alpha's Choice
Book 3: Mated in Mist

Book 4: Wolf Betrayed

Book 5: Fractured Silence

Book 6: Destiny Disgraced

Book 7: Eternal Mourning

Book 8: Strength Enduring

Book 9: Forever Broken

The Elements of Five Series:

Book 1: From Breath and Ruin

Book 2: From Flame and Ash

Book 3: From Spirit and Binding

Book 4: From Shadow and Silence

The Branded Pack Series:
(Written with Alexandra Ivy)

Book 1: Stolen and Forgiven

Book 2: Abandoned and Unseen

Book 3: Buried and Shadowed

Dante's Circle Series:

Book 1: Dust of My Wings

Book 2: Her Warriors' Three Wishes

Book 3: An Unlucky Moon

Book 3.5: His Choice

Book 4: Tangled Innocence

Book 5: Fierce Enchantment

Book 6: An Immortal's Song

Book 7: Prowled Darkness

Book 8: Dante's Circle Reborn

Holiday, Montana Series:

Book 1: Charmed Spirits

Book 2: Santa's Executive

Book 3: Finding Abigail

Book 4: Her Lucky Love

Book 5: Dreams of Ivory

The Happy Ever After Series:

Flame and Ink

Ink Ever After

Single Title:

Finally Found You

CPSIA information can be obtained
at www.ICGtesting.com
Printed in the USA
BVHW041020021120
592327BV00008B/337